STO

FRIENDS
OF ACPL

3 1833 03075 8111

Fiction
Dressler, Mylene, 1963-
The medusa tree

7-25-97

D0966004

ALLEN COUNTY PUBLIC LIBRARY
FORT WAYNE, INDIANA 46802

You may return this book to any location of
the Allen County Public Library

DEMCO

The Medusa Tree

The Medusa Tree

Mylène Dressler

MacMurray & Beck
Denver/Aspen

Copyright © 1997 by Mylène Dressler
Published by:
MacMurray & Beck, Inc.
1649 Downing Street
Denver, Colorado 80218

All rights reserved. No part of this book may be reproduced or transmitted
in any form or by any means, electronic or mechanical, including photo-
copying, recording, or any information stroage and retrieval system,
without written permission from the publisher, except for the inclusion of
brief quotations in a review.

Printed and bound in the United States of America

1   2   3   4   5   6   7   8   9   10

Library of Congress Cataloging-in-Publication Data
Dressler, Mylène, 1963–
    The medusa tree : a novel / by Mylène Dressler.
      p.   cm.
    ISBN 1–878448–75–7
    I. Title.
PS3554.R432M43   1997
813'.54—dc21   96–45547
                                          CIP

MacMurray & Beck Fiction; General Editor, Greg Michalson
The Medusa Tree designed by Laurie Dolphin.
The text was designed and set in Walbaum by Stacia Schaefer.

Publisher's Note: This is a work of fiction. Names, characters, places, and
incidents either are the product of the author's imagination or are used fic-
titiously. Any resemblance to actual events, locales, or persons, living or
dead, is entirely coincidental.

Allen County Public Library
900 Webster Street
PO Box 2270
Fort Wayne

For Dennis

My grandmothers' faces look out from behind the screened porch cautiously, like two nuns ready to leap back into their old habits.

"Oh *dag, kind! Dag!*"

"*Dag* Marget!"

Whatever has been happening inside, whatever tables have been lifted off their legs, cups and spoons floated around the room, cards shuffled of their own accord, or secret knowledges exchanged, my grandmothers settle them down again and come out, smiling, with upturned hands to greet me, into the Northern California sunlight that turns the dust on their skins a faint, sparkling orange.

"*Dag* Gerda! *Dag* Fan!"

I kiss them, tasting the familiar chemical mixture of salt and powder on their cheeks. My grandmothers'

1

faces are soft and folding, like fallen peaches. Their fists, hardened with age, push me up onto the porch and inside the house, their knuckles digging sharply between my shoulder blades. My grandmothers like to show their strength these days. They push and slap and poke, as if to say, Hey you, you are young, you are flexible, you can still take whatever we have left to give out to you. Gerda doesn't push as much as Fan, because Gerda is older and so much the stronger of the two of them. It's Fanny who has always had to push to be felt, to be heard, because Gerda can be so overpowering.

Gerda is using a cane to walk around now. She's short, hunched, and has the look of an old fighter. She stands as if she's hanging a little underneath her clothing: a man's shirt over polyester pants. She smiles at me from under her curled black hair, out from under the bridge of her painted eyebrows, while Fanny, in her gilded Indonesian *kabaya*, stands taller, thinner, slightly faded behind her.

Fanny was the great beauty between them. Her moon face is still held up by high cheekbones. Gerda's face is plain and flat. Her cane is the excuse I've used to come out here.

"Sit down," Gerda says briskly. "Fanny will go bring us some coffee."

In the living room things appear to be in their usual places. In front of the pulled curtains sit their prim Danish loveseat and chairs, wooden-armed and elbowing, brought over from Holland long after the war. Above the television hangs an old clock, pointed around

2

the edges like a compass or star. Some of Corinne's cheap brass candlesticks scale from small to large on the false brick mantel. Dusty bottles of airplane liquor crowd the rollaway bar. Only a few gleams of elegance are left: a gold wall lizard, called a *tjitjak*, a lucky charm, gift from my mother brought back from Indonesia after one of her many travels; and a few watercolors and sketches done by Gerda's dead husband. Palazzi in Venice. A spired church in The Hague. They hover, unsure of themselves in their American home.

My other grandmother comes in from the kitchen on geisha steps. Her batik rustles softly as she walks. Floating in front of her are the translucent cups and saucers that are so like her. Fragile. Egg-thin. She sets them down, fills them with java, then sits back beside Gerda inside the loveseat. Fanny's eyes are watery, sleepy with age. But she smiles at me, because she is glad to see me. Or at least she might be, if I could ever see anything behind the veil of those dreamy looks.

"So," Gerda says, slurping her coffee, the china dwarfed in her creased hand. "Drink."

My mother called me last week from her hotel in Belgium.

"Gerda wants to have it done," she repeated distractedly. (The connection was good that day; her voice sounded close, brittle.) "The procedure," she hurried. "That thing, that replacement surgery she's been wanting. I told her, What do you want to go and put yourself

3

through all that pain for? What are you thinking you'll still do? Wimbledon? But of course there's no talking to her."

Mama sighed as though exhausted—a sign she was getting ready to avoid strain. "We can't leave Fan alone like that while Gerda's in the hospital, Marget. You know what Fan is, she's just—helpless. If anything happens—if anything happens she won't be able to go on. And then you know someone has to watch out for Corinne. You know how she's always snooping around, looking over their things, like she can't wait to get Gerda out of the way. Your father and I are going to be out here for at least another two months. . . . So what do you think, hon? Can you go, when your season is over? Can you go out, and have a look at them? I hate to interrupt your life this way, I'm sure you have big plans—but can you get a flight out next week? La Guardia is best. And please don't say anything about that I, that we, it's just. You know. I'm getting vibrations. And hon. Please let us pay . . . ?"

My mother's concern had trailed off, reaching blindly. My near-sounding, distant mother is like a hand in the dark, groping to tie our loose ends. My mother is often away.

I hung up the telephone, stared at the walls of my apartment, and thought suddenly of my grandmothers. It was like coming upon an iceberg. Huge. Simple. I could see myself drifting along with them for a week, a month, aimless, spellbound, sharing with them their anonymous piece of California coast.

Sitting now beside them, with my battered flight bags piled in stumps around my knees, I can see how much I might be able to help them—how much my grandmothers might really need me. How busy they've been, applying pencil to their shrinking eyes! Curling their thinning hairdos, tightly, getting their lipsticks just right. My grandmothers are trying, they are staying. Even though they are hiding themselves, they are demanding something, they are making themselves plain, they want to be seen. All I have to do is notice them, and I can go unnoticed here myself.

My grandmothers look at me. East and West mingle in their faces: circle, conflict, dance, and merge. In Fan the effect is harmony. In her half-moon Indies eyes lurk melodies to charm the still, Dutch face. But in Gerda the Dutch and Javanese features war, turning flat, broad, plain, irreconcilable.

We sit and say nothing, sipping our coffees, facing each other like three pyramids searching our neighbors for cracks.

Chapter Two

I drop my bags upstairs in their guest bedroom.

On the wall above the bed are photos of each of the three of us. I nudge my suitcase aside and sit near the headboard, staring at my own image first. I can't help it. I feel some distant responsibility for that gangling girl, seven years old, grimacing in her pale pink tutu. Her little eyes are so wide, her eyebrows so arched, her hair pulled back so tightly she could feel the skin giving way under her ears. My mother is in the next frame, posing at seventeen. Here she is a young woman I never knew, with a voluptuous body in a scoop-necked leotard.

Mama's was a lovely arabesque.

Fanny stands alone in the last gilded frame, nearly naked underneath her Grecian costume. She trails a white scarf over one bony knee. Gerda took this picture

6

in Holland after the war. You can see it: the affection in the angle. Very few pictures survive of my grandmother before then, few pictures, that is, of Fanny when she was young. I asked Gerda about it once, when Fan was out of the room. But Gerda had whispered only, "Well, and what? You don't think they kept pictures for her, do you, in a terrible place like that?"

Across the hall is my grandmothers' bedroom. Everything in it is open. It is Fan's terrible fear of odors. The windows are flung wide, the chests, the sliding closet doors. I see neat double peaks of brassieres, folds of white underwear, shelves of shining purses over hangered rows of polyester pants. Gerda's beige girdles, embarrassing for their size, hang to dry on a wooden rack beside the window. A breeze ruffles through the room. The girdles rise and fall, swinging like gates.

On one nightstand is a picture of Gerda's dead husband, Rollie. Rollie sits astride a sweating black horse. A small Malay boy holds his bridle. Rollie's face is blond and wan and damp under his pith helmet. He is young and handsome, already hollowed by his disease. He was a proper Dutch colonial. On Fanny's side of the bed there are no pictures of a husband, only a miniature Swiss grandfather clock ticking faintly, like a watch. No place there for him, for Han, for the young man who abandoned her and my baby mother all those years ago to join, of all things (Mama used to hiss the word), a *circus*.

Now I'm older I think I know how the old man must have felt. Wife and baby waiting for him, right after the long, terrible war. Right after the blood and muck of the

Burmese jungles, right after the years of sweat and labor, and then, when it's all over, and you suddenly find yourself free . . .

Now my grandfather lives in Johannesburg. He has servants again, and an Afrikaner wife. He sends letters to me once a month. He seems quite happy.

Growing up, I didn't think it was anything special that my grandmothers slept together. It was only, after all, what all adults did, and what children were sometimes allowed to do, for practice. Then, when I grew old enough to imagine such things but still young enough to ask, my mother had explained to me, surprised, looking up from the giant green parrot she sat embroidering. "You have to remember, Marget, they were just two lonely women, by themselves, when they were younger. And it was during the Second World War, and the men were gone, and they didn't have anybody to rely on. So they were afraid. They kept together for comfort. That's all."

I understood. I understand. In my family, we don't like to name things. We prefer to keep them hidden, cocooned, folded away in shut drawers. Even today I don't believe in that story of loneliness—that story that Gerda and Fan were two unlucky old maids. I can't believe love is only a long, secret fear. Only an accident that hits you and tars you together.

Perhaps, if I tiptoe carefully downstairs, I can catch my grandmothers as they really must be when they're alone, whirling things in the air of a room without me.

Downstairs, my grandmothers sit quietly together, side by side on the Danish loveseat. They are watching television, and don't even seem to notice each other. A tennis match is on—Gerda's sport. She turns her flat, quarrelsome face toward me and smiles.

"Sit down, *kind*, sit down!" Her Dutch accent is slurred and hard and rich. She beats a warm place for me on the chair beside them.

Fan turns beautiful sleepy eyes to me, and smiles.

"Poof! Look at that!" Gerda jerks a blunt finger toward the television. "That woman is afraid to come up to the net. She is afraid to come up to the net! You can't be afraid, I tell you. It's stupid. Stupid! Look, *toch*, that's why I miss my girl, that's why I miss my Chrissie so much. Did you see that? You stupid Italian! You deserved that! Ha! Well, nobody can beat Martina. Nobody has her speed. But still. You have to be a little more aggressive, I think.

"So!" she says again, when she has finished with the set and can give her full attention to me, beaming. "How are you now, *kind?* Everything is good upstairs? Fan makes everything good? Ja. You look real, real good. What do you think, Fan? Ja? No. You are too thin, she says. I think so too. Maybe they like you to dance too hard out there."

Fan nods her head as if in time to music. Fanny is my real grandmother, my mother's mother. She isn't a forceful or vocal person, and only smiles her place in most conversations, so that sometimes I've had to pretend I have Gerda's blood pumping in my veins, powerful, noisy, hard to overlook.

9

"What do you eat?" Gerda asks curiously, looking at my stomach.

"The usual. Candy bars. Coca-Cola. Potato chips."

"Hmph! Not funny. And not enough, I think. You look pale, *kind*. And hungry. How old are you?"

"Twenty-two." It feels so shallow. Like one of those chafing dishes you might have gotten at a bridal shower.

"Ha!" Gerda laughs, rocking back on the loveseat and gripping her swollen knees. "Ja. That is a good age! I remember that age. You feel strong. You begin to know yourself, to *feel* yourself, almost. You begin to feel your power. Hey?" I nod. Gerda is eighty-one. She's hard to resist.

"Fan!" she shouts. "Hey, Fan! Why don't you go now and get us some cookies?"

My grandmother rises and slips wordlessly to the kitchen.

"So then," Gerda continues. "You tell me about your trip."

She leans forward on her cane, listening attentively, like a bat, absorbing me with every line in her silver-haired face. Fan patters softly in the kitchen, in the background.

"Like a shadow!" My mother used to throw up her hands, disgusted.

After a minute I can feel the strain in my throat. The slight pull and tear as I speak. I notice this painful tugging whenever I'm around them. But I recognize it: I'm shouting so Fanny can hear me.

She comes in finally, smiling, balancing a plate of fresh butter cookies in her hands.

10

"Eat eat eat!" she sings. Her voice is high, fluted.

"So," Gerda says again, waiting for Fanny to sit beside her and to fold her magnetic fingers, quietly. "When did you talk to your mama last? I don't understand. I don't know exactly what she is doing over there. Why are your parents now in Brussels?"

"Antwerp!" My grandmother pokes Gerda in the ribs.

"Antwerp! What are they buying now?"

"Daddy's looking into a moving company. A Belgian one."

Gerda frowns.

"*Nee.* I tell you what, *kind.* Your parents are getting too rich. It's too many houses, too many cars, too much business. Bah! If you're not careful it will all fall on top of you, like in the Indies. It's dangerous. And then also," she switches to her professional tone, "it isn't always so good for the taxes."

She studies her thumbs, knocking them together like hammers.

"What kind of a company, you say?"

"Moving company. Moving things. They want to ship containers, all over the world. Daddy thinks it goes with his warehouses. Mama is looking at a place in France, she wants to buy an old farmhouse or something. Anyway," I rush on when I see their blank expressions, "they're just waiting until everything gets settled. That's all." I take a cookie, but can't bring myself to bite into it.

My grandmothers sit looking into me, helpless. It's as though they're trying to reach her, through me.

"What! A moving company? They should, the way they are always moving. Dallas. Nairobi. Now Brussels. Bah! What did we do to her, I should like to know, that she always has to be going so far away from us? We gave her everything, I tell you. Like Corinne. And now she doesn't come to see us. All this moving around. It's ridiculous. I shouldn't like it."

"But how are *you?*" I smile at both of them, to change the subject. "You both look good!"

Gerda looks at me sharply.

"What does she tell you, your mama?"

Fan leans and pinches me above the knee. Hard.

"She wanted me to help you out for your operation. But I told her there was nothing to worry about. I told her I didn't think you needed my help."

"That's right!" Gerda turns to my grandmother. "Tell this old one here that, too! I know exactly what I'm doing. I don't need help! It's only ridiculous for me, this pain. It's stupid, this going around like a cripple. I'm not ninety yet." She shakes her butter cookie at us, like a talisman.

"The doctors can fix almost anything you ask. It's really wonderful, Marget. My doctor is going to give me all new knees, made of steel. He says there will be no problem, only they will have to be careful for the— how do you say?—the anesthesia. Bah!" She turns again to Fan. "You wait until I am finished. Then you will see."

"Oh, Vent." My grandmother frowns, using her pet name for Gerda. "*Ik . . . ik weet het niet.*"

"What do you mean you don't know? *I* know. Go now, and make us some dinner. Marget, you come into the backyard. I want to show you my roses."

She unlocks the sliding patio door and sets it carefully aside. Gerda seems to feel she must watch her strength or risk tearing the house down.

Their garden is meager, depressing, especially in comparison to the one they kept back in the old house, the big house—back when they lived in the valley, back when everything that was Gerda's and Fan's was as huge and ordered and bordered as a country that flew its own flag.

Now Gerda's neighbors crowd around her with swing sets and sagging fences and rusting basketball poles and hairy, unmanaged pines. She has just enough room for the one bank of enormous, radiant roses, bending, drooping, nearly toppling from their own weight. I finger their white and yellow and red petticoats.

Gerda bends carefully on her cane, to fill her face with one of them.

"Ah!" she breathes.

"They're gorgeous, Gerda. Just beautiful."

"Ja, *bedankt*. See over here my apple. Small but good, very tasty." She pulls a young pippin from the tree.

"Did you plant those there, or did they just come up?"

"What? Oh. The little blue flowers. No, I don't know. They just came to me. On the wind. When anything comes to me that way, you know, I keep it. I take care of it."

She turns, squinting, to look at the house.

"So what were you dancing before you came here?" she asks.

"*Giselle*," I answer too quickly.

"Ah! I know that one." She nods. "Where the girls who die of their broken hearts come back to dance their young men to death, at night. Ha! It's a good one. We also had such ghost stories, in my youth. Are you the star, then, of this ballet?"

"No, no." It would have been nice. Giselle goes stark raving mad at the end of Act One, pulling her hair out. She accuses the man who has deceived her, waving his sword at him, then has a heart attack and drops dead. No more problems.

"You still like dancing," Gerda says certainly.

"Of course."

This isn't exactly untrue. You do something long enough, it gets inside you. Then it's too late. It isn't a question, anymore, of whether you love it.

"I made demi-soloist before I got—I made demi-soloist."

"Hey, that's good, isn't it? Fan will be so happy. She loves your dancing, you know. She is just like you. We are so proud. We only wish that is what your mama could have done. But of course, it was impossible."

We stare at our toes.

"It's a hard life for a person, sometimes?"

"Yes."

"I thought so much."

She straightens her back and heaves and slaps me soundly across mine.

"Ha! I never went in for dancing myself, Marget. Fan tried to teach me. But I like sport better. No music. Just rhythm. Just—the body."

Her eyes glitter.

"You still miss it, Gerda?"

"Oh, ja! Oh yes, yes. I played until I was in my forties, you know. In the Indies, at first. Tennis was a big game. But also in Holland, after the war. I loved it. I was what you would call a real, real amateur. I wouldn't change that, you know, even though now—except I was born too soon—I could have made so much money. But these new people, these stars, I don't know. Look at McEnroe. I don't know if he loves the sport. It's like a business to him. An advertisement. When you become a professional, something about you dies, I think. The love, maybe."

Maybe Gerda is right. Maybe life isn't all a mistake, at twenty-two, just because you stop loving the one thing you know how to do. But—how do you start over? Do you have to throw it all out with the bathwater? Because, at twenty-two, you have to wonder: how much will I have left?

"And you were a champion," I prod, to keep her thinking about herself.

"Oh, yes. Yes! I was champion of the whole, whole, archipelago." She breathes the word out. "I played with men, you know. I beat them. Have I told you about the general? The Japanese general who made me play for them, during the war?"

Good.

"With those flags," she nods her head. "With those little yellow flags, blowing on the front of his car."

She tucks the trunk of her arm more deeply into mine. We walk a few steps. Now I am safe. Now she no longer sees me.

Chapter Three

What I remember first is a man sitting very straight in a chair. Smoking a pipe. Biting down on it. His eyes are keen.

The head of this man, my grandfather, is bald, and spotted as if from the red pits of fallen berries. He wears a tweed coat, like an old British schoolmaster. He is turkey-chinned. He is sullen. He is old.

At the top of the chair, his armchair, around him, wrapping around him, is a cat. The cat is gray and white. The gray pattern of the chair is underneath the gray cat, and the white pattern of a square window rises behind the gray chair. My grandfather leans forward, rimmed in light, but doesn't see me. I think this might be because he isn't real. Probably I've simply pieced him together out of old dreams and talk and images from photo albums.

This man whom I see sitting in the chair is my father's father. Not the father of my mother, not the man who left Fanny and my baby mother all those years ago to join, of all things, a circus. This is my other grandfather, the one who died of a heart attack soon after I was born. My grandmother, my father's mother, survived him long enough to become another, more trustworthy memory. She too was stained like a cherry bowl around the ears, and also nearly bald; but her best feature was her double plate of false teeth, which she could slide out of her mouth and chatter like a pair of castanets in front of her face. It was horrible, this chattering, and I asked her to do it often. Then she died, and all her horribleness was lost to me. And so I had nothing more to do with my father's family.

Next I am in my parents' house. There is record music, waltzing. The trilling of pianos. And books, so many, reclining like the spines of old animals inside the shelves. Some had pictures, of white women with huge dresses like balloons and bare, snow-white arms and pointed, black-buckled slippers. Others housed kings and queens, collared, wearing dinner plates around their necks. Still others were filled with sad, ruined buildings made of stone, stone statues and faces and horses and men.

Often, after looking together into such terrible and beautiful books, which much later I learned were her favorite histories, my mother and I would sit together solemnly, patiently, and she would stare into some faraway place I couldn't see. She would sit and stare over her coffee, her wrist over the open page, dreaming herself into those books.

In those days my parents hadn't yet come across the fortune that would come to them years later. We lived in a modest, one-story California house of blue stucco; Mama stayed home with me during the day, while my father went into the city. On some days, for a treat, he took me in with him to see the tall black bank building where he worked. From his window I could see the traffic crawling in the street below us; if we turned and craned we could just catch a glimpse of the beautiful Golden Gate, resting one of its wings on a chunk of mountain. That high up I felt giddy, invincible. In the elevator going down I jumped and jumped, just to feel the carpeted floor giving out underneath me.

On the freeway going home I counted the cars called bugs, and in the parks we passed I counted the people called hippies. Daddy made me put my hand down. He said it wasn't safe to point at them.

When I got old enough to walk to the end of our street, I could stand and watch the fog roll in from the bay. I could see it come creeping over the hills in a blind froth, across the highway and into our clean, new, bare neighborhood, gobbling up each corner and each matching pastel house, one by one, until it wrapped itself around me in a cold, sticky embrace. In this way I learned time.

On clear days, I studied airplanes. Planes, I knew, were large and heavy. Yet they flew. I was small and light, and I couldn't fly. To fly, then, I must be heavy. I went into the garage and squeezed into an old backpack the heaviest things I could find. A hammer. A red brick. An empty milk bottle. A piece of rotten firewood. I was something, with my heavy pack behind me. I took up more space, more weight, more importance in the world. Then if the fog was still blowing in torn sheets through our street, I would go down to the corner and run. And jump. And jump. And jump. With all my might. And only once and for the barest instant did my back fit into an invisible hand that came up from underneath me, a hard gust that picked me up and carried me, a flying ball, across two long cracks in the white sidewalk. Afterwards I couldn't make anyone believe I had taken off. But from this I learned that a thing will usually happen in just exactly the opposite way of what you would expect of it.

I was five years old when I discovered I was beautiful. This came as a shock. For me the most beautiful girl in the world lived on the next street, and her name, like a bell, was Anna Wong. Anna's parents were Chinese. Her round cheeks and round body were completely smooth, like she had no bones. Her eyes were dark and clear like oily black beads, and her hair was cut like a doll's into a perfectly straight line across her forehead. My mother would never cut my hair evenly that way. She thought it looked too perfect, so she broke the line of my short dark bangs, snipping in ragged jags with her silver scissors. I always looked as if the hem of my head were unraveling.

I worshipped Anna because she was perfect. I told her again and again how incredibly beautiful I thought she was. This gave Anna a real sense of distinction and made her very careful about her appearance. Once, while we were playing jump-rope with some of the other girls on our street, something happened and the red handle at one end flew off like a missile and hit Anna, hard, right in her face. Oh! Oh! Does it hurt! we all yelled, and we hurried to circle and soothe her. We stood in front of Anna, apologetic, just as if she were a torn Mona Lisa. Then her little pearl fists came down from her tearless face. No! she shouted at us. No! But was there any mark on her? Was there any mark?

I couldn't play with Anna after that. She was too disgusting. But later that same year the school photographer called my mother to ask if I could pose for a pajama ad. Mama said no. Ladies in red smocks at the grocery store started to bend down and pinch and tickle me, and the Avon Lady who came to our house with her perfume and eye shadows and hand creams groped, as though I were a ten-carat bracelet underwater. And after they had all stooped to coddle and tweak and prod me, and after Mama had pulled me back away from them, circling my neck with her hand—then I began to believe it. I couldn't stop walking by mirrors, to see the beautiful creature turning to look back at me from her passing coach. I got into the habit of seeing myself twisted around that way, even when the mirror wasn't there.

My mother, I later found out, wasn't beautiful. But my grandmother, the quiet one, was. In this way I learned a sense of proportion.

The next year Mama got a job at a Swedish deli-bakery in Oakland. We needed the money, she explained carefully to me, for a storage business Daddy was starting. So I was going to be stored at my grandmothers' house, after school and during the long summer vacation.

We got up while it was still dark and the fog was clinging in blue muffs to the ears of the street lamps. We drove sometimes by the bakery first, where I stood far apart, shivering nervously, from the fat vat of oil full of boiling doughnuts. The man who watched over the hot grease looked up from his newspaper, and smiled at me. So did Dora and Carmen in their smudged and bloody aprons, lifting me up under the armpits and groaning, joking with me, and then afterwards (when they thought I wasn't looking) wiping my greasy hand-prints off the bottom of the glass counters, where I had left them in pairs like streaky moths' wings. And yet the bakery was a terrible place. What I dreaded more than anything was Mama getting her hands caught in the whirling meat slicers. I had nightmares, her arms held out to me like stumps, dripping blood.

My grandmothers' house wasn't far from the bakery, just over the hills and down in the valley that smelled of wild mustard seed and gasoline and burnt grass. I had nothing to do at their house except to play all day and eat what Fan told me to eat, whenever and wherever she told me to eat it. Gerda still worked long hours in those days as an accountant for a local milk company. It was Fanny's job to keep the house clean and neat, to cook all the meals, to do all the laundry, and to make sure I didn't touch any of the sockets or any shocking part of my body.

Fanny couldn't drive a car; she seldom left the house. It was Gerda who went out alone into the world, to make all the money that, I sensed, really kept everything seamlessly running. Gerda's force was breathed into every line and fold of the big, old house. She fertilized and mowed all the wide, lush lawns, she designed the sweeping flower beds, she cultivated the fruit orchard, she built a gazebo and a sunroom and a huge, screened back porch. Gerda had bought the old house, their second in this country, for the two of them to be alone in together. It wasn't old at all, really, just an ordinary ranch-style home from the 1950s. But Gerda kept adding on to it, as if she could never wall in enough of the free space around her. One day, my father said, shaking his head, the place was going to be way too much for them.

Fanny had a sharper eye in those days. There was no half-eaten sandwich she wouldn't find, eventually, crushed and hidden in a napkin in a wastepaper basket; and when I was busy taking my nap on my cot in Gerda's "office" room, surrounded by adding machines and spools of flecked paper and rubbing myself, frantically, to start the fire I wanted to put out, nothing would stop her from coming in to catch me, clicking her tongue, and then throwing open all the windows with a swift, strong emotion.

"Body odor!" she would gasp with a brief, faint strength. Then she would disappear to check on her pantry, and arrange and rearrange the shelves of canned food they had stored and hoarded together, Gerda and

Fanny, to avoid any new disaster that might befall them, even in America.

On rainy days I had to stay inside or play on the enclosed back porch. This room felt like an invisible, slumbering animal, caged in a moss-colored screen. It was a shady, moody, wild place—tropical, green-lit, hung with wiry asparagus fern and spider plants and blue-streaked wandering Jews, half-furnished with white wicker tables and tan peacock chairs, looking deserted, scattered, as if people had hurriedly gotten up and left them. A yellow fly strip hung down from the fiberglass roof that sounded like drums when the rains beat on it. The fly strip was Fan's doing. The insects stuck neatly to it, struggled, and died out of reach.

On sunny days I played in the orchard under the peaches, pears, plums, and apricots; the smaller trees were oranges and lemons. There were two almond trees, whose mysterious furred fruits turned imperceptibly into hard, pocked nuts. The birches got the worst of me. The three of them stood off alone in a corner, sequestered, elegant, bowing. I circled them, mumbling strange, half-made-up songs, then rushed them with my fingernails, peeling back their parchment skins.

At the old house Gerda's roses were everywhere. In the corners, creeping over the fences, lolling next to the redwood gazebo, climbing up the back of the garden shed. One bunch I thought of as Oma Fan's Roses, because Gerda had planted them right outside the kitchen window, where Fanny could see them, and because they were all white and dusty and more delicate than the

24

rest. I posed for Easter pictures with them, in a bonnet and pink dress, with my big pink sugar egg with frosted writing on one side that read, To A Very Special Girl.

Gerda wasn't a girl. That much I knew. She was big, and loud, and strong, and she wore plain clothes. Her dark hair was cut short, and her thick hands were tough, like an elephant's. She was of course some sort of man. I saw that she did the things my father did, saw that she wasn't pretty like Fan, and filled in the rest. Gerda was a man who wore lipstick. She was not exactly like my father, but she wasn't exactly like Fan or my mother, either. She was a man-woman. Mama, I had asked one day, just to be certain, isn't Gerda a man, only different?

Mama got angry.

"Of course not! What a silly question, Marget! It's just that she likes to wear pants all the time. You should know that. Gerda is not a man, she's a woman, and she is like your grandmother, only she's not really related to you. Fan is your real grandmother, but Gerda is not."

It was a double blow that morning. Gerda was not a man. Gerda was not related to me, she was not, my mother explained, of the same family. Mama said these things as if they were real. I cried. What was Gerda doing, then, with us? How could she, in one day, be both not a man, and not in our family? I couldn't make my mother understand that it was like two bright pins stuck on a wall, and that pulling them out had made the picture I knew fall down, down, down. Gerda was not a man. Gerda was not in our family. I looked at Gerda the next day, to see if it made any difference. She seemed the same. But I noticed for the first time the curves under her blouse.

Later in the summer, on weekends, when her orchard was full and hanging, Gerda would invite some of her neighbors to help us with the harvest. We climbed up into the branches with our shining metal buckets, bought at Sears, then handed them down loaded to Fanny or my mother, who poured the fruit into plastic washing baskets. Once, when I was ten years old and just beginning to wear my hair long and with a part down the middle like the women in the magazines, Gerda and I climbed into the same tree. It was leaf-smelling, wine purple, a full, luscious plum.

Gerda was a large woman—I understood that now—and sat comfortably on the thickest branches. Her rough hands pulled the tender fruits off in threes and fours. My hands worked more slowly, savoring, each time, the tug, the short resistance, then—ping!—the warm weight in my palm. After a few minutes Gerda stopped and looked down at me. She took my hand by the wrist, and opened it. In the center of my palm she placed a perfect, moon-split plum.

"Ja," she smiled.

Then she covered my hand with her own, forcing my fingers to close, tightly, forcing my fingers to fist and squeeze until the crushed red juices ran bloody and sweet down our arms.

"Do you feel that, *kind?*" she said excitedly over the howling pain in my fingers. "Do you feel it?"

I was frightened of Gerda. Of her flat, savage face, of her narrow, pocketed eyes—though she only laughed easily and helped me down from the tree, wiping my arm fleshily with her own.

"Fan!" she called briskly. "Fan! Hey! You! A towel over here, please!"

"Ja, *toch, even wachten*," my younger grandmother had grumbled, busy filling her baskets and not really paying attention.

Gerda sits in one of her curved iron garden chairs. She breathes deeply and settles satisfied into herself. Her eyes have gone small, far, and back.

"So you see," she continues, looking up at me, "the best thing is always to do what you are told. Sit, *kind*. Me, I did anything the Japanese wanted. Anything. They hated me, the Dutch women, for it. But I am not Dutch. I am Dutch-Indonesian. They looked down on us, the Dutch, and we looked down on them, the Indonesians. Oh, it wasn't smart, you know, the way we all treated the Indonesians.

"But the Dutch women hated me especially, because I did anything the Japanese told me to do. I said to them, 'Yes yes!' and I bowed. I bowed twice. That was the most respect you could show. I bowed twice to them, very low, and the Japanese, they bowed only once. They took over the whole country, during the war. You know? They took Java. And Borneo. Sumatra. Where were the Americans? I should like to have asked. Where were the Australians? Where were the British? I was running around, saying yes yes. I was bowing like crazy.

"They put me to work as an accountant when they took the sugar factories. And I did it. They made me give them tennis lessons, and I did it. I had no choice—it was either play or go to the prison camps, where many Dutch women were being sent. And after our games they gave me their tennis shoes to clean like a coolie, to carry through the streets to the man in the shoe shop. I didn't do it. I spit on those shoes, I tell you. I spit on them, and I cleaned them, at night, at home, and I kept the money they gave me to pay to the shoemaker. You have to be smart in a war, Marget. You have no choice. Not when you have hungry people to feed. I had Fanny and your baby mama in my house and both my sisters, Elly and Pip.

"And those Dutch women. We saw them later, going in trucks to the prison camps. They had called me names on the street. But I did whatever I was told to do. I said to myself, I want to live. I am a person for living.

"Then, one day, one of the *kampong* boys comes running down our street, shouting that a big black auto is coming, a big black auto with yellow flags on the front of it. And he is shouting because he knows everyone in the street must stop and turn and bow to this car, and he wants to see the bowing, he thinks it is all a game, because he's young and he doesn't know his sisters have already been taken to work as prostitutes for the army. Ayo! this boy shouts to us. Ayo! And I'm thinking to myself, Now they have come. Now they have come for me, to take my house away, and I am stupid because even though I have done everything they tell me, still they always come in the end, to get you.

"So. I stand at the door. I am thinking: You will not take my house. You cannot know this house, Marget. It is not like anything you would see here. Or in Holland. This house, it was like, it was like—I can't express it. You would have to know the Indies. Or my husband. But anyway, I am thinking, while this car is coming toward me down the street: I will not let you take me. You will have to catch me first, and then I will bite you, and hit you, and so you will have to kill me. Because now I am a person for *fighting*. But this auto, it comes right up the drive to my door, right up to me with all its little yellow flags flying. Yellow was the color of the Javanese princes. And then a little driver comes out, and he opens the door, and then a general comes out, looking like he hates having to wait for such a lowly man.

"I recognize this general. He is in charge over the sugar factory where I work. General Kabuto is his name. So the factory is how he knows where to find me, I think, the factory is how he knows all about me. He stood there on my porch with his little mustache on his nothing-face, oh I remember that face, I remember that nothing-face very well. And this Kabuto, he says to me:

"'Gerda Wilhelmina Van Doorn?'

"'Yes,' I say, bowing. I am looking like this at the floor. Because you are not supposed to look at them in their faces.

"'I am here to request your participation in the next Pan-Asiatic tennis tournament, representing the District of Surabaya.' We spoke English, you see. Even though they wanted us to speak Japanese.

"'But sir,' I tell him, 'sir, it is not possible. I am out of practice.' I don't want to play for him—him, that nothing-man! That is what they want, a play, a show, to show the world how much we love them, how so very happy we are in our new Co-Prosperity Sphere. That is what they call us!

"But this man, this Kabuto, he is smart. He knows already everything about me. He says, 'You are lying.' He points to my arm. He says, 'You are in practice. You are playing every week in the officers' club.'

"'Yes sir,' I say. 'But it is the level of your officers. It is so low.'

"Hoo! He wanted to kick me, he was standing on one leg! But he didn't. 'Never mind!' he says. 'You will play! And Mrs. Van Doorn—' and he says this very carefully to me, he leans forward, showing his teeth, like this, so I can tell he doesn't like what he is having to say:

"'You will win.'"

Gerda leans forward, her eyes shining dangerously into mine. It's eerie, almost enough to make me want to jump away. But in the next moment the face of the general is fading from her own.

"So," she leans back again. "So. I bow to him. I bow twice, like this, very low. He bows only once, very short. Then he goes. And there it is. I can say nothing against this match. I can do nothing against such an order. I'm only glad I have kept my house and family—for now. But then I begin to think. But Gerda, I say to myself. Do you really think you can win? Do you really think you can play for these men, for these stupid, little, yellow, greasy men? But yes, I say to myself. *Yes.* Always I like to win. Ever since I was a little girl. So I decide then: I am going to win. Only for me. Because I love it."

Her eyes close. Her memories must be weaving through her now, like an old, intimate friend. I sit back, drowsing along with her. I don't really know much about the Indies. Mama doesn't remember. My father has English and Welsh blood. It all feels like something behind a curtain somewhere: but the fly-ropes are broken and the gold tassels are all gnawed, and beyond, in the dark, something shapeless moves. Still, if I wanted to I could let Gerda carry me away. Take me off to someplace green and unfamiliar, soothing, foreign. Not Marget. I imagine a woman, young, sturdy and strong, see the sweeping curve of her body in motion. I see her darting back and forth across the earthen court, her patches of sweat, her muscle, her expert hands, her nimble legs. People above in the galleries, white linen in the heat and shade. The net. The opponent. The dividing line. Blinding. There is the opening. I reach in. I strain for the return—

"Ah!"

Gerda's eyes stare, two inches from my face. She has leapt, sitting forward, I don't know how, while I was dozing, and curled her fingers around my wrist, holding me in place like the shaft of a racket. She grins at me, knowingly. Triumphant.

"And so!" she says at last, letting go. "I beat those men. Every one. From Borneo, and Sumatra, and Balikpapan. Japanese. All of them. I even beat my biggest rival, a

Japanese from the district of Jakarta. But now you must listen, Marget, because this is the rest of it. Now is when I really win and I know that no one can ever beat me. When I am finished, and everyone in the stands is clapping, very softly, just like birds, then I am given the silver trophy cup, the one I won't get to keep, and then I am told I must turn and bow to them, especially to the men at the top. So I did it. But when it was over I looked up at them, the princes and generals, right in their faces. That Kabuto, he was handing people cigars. He saw me, and then he wasn't smiling anymore. He was looking at me—how can I call it?—with a kind of stone face. And do you know why, *kind?* It is because I won for him. It is because he could not have this day without my winning.

"But then," she says excitedly, twisting inside her chair, "but then, the next day, when I am home again, the little boy comes running once more from the *kampong*. Ayo! he cries. Ayo! And here comes the black auto again with its little yellow flags down our street. But this time I don't wait at the door. I go and sit in my big chair on the porch, and I listen to the sound of that auto. And I hear when it comes up, and I hear the sound of the driver when he opens the general's door, but still I don't go, I don't move an inch, until I hear the driver pull our bell. And only then, slowly, I get up and answer it. Fanny and Elly and Pip are already in the hallway. They are so frightened I can feel them shaking through the floor. But I say nothing, I just go and open the door to the general, standing there, and he says nothing to me, just standing. We just wait, looking—you know—very uncertainly at each other. I see he looks a little unhappy.

"And then slowly, very slowly, he bows to me. Twice. Very low, like this."

She kowtows.

"And then I bow, just once. Only a little. Like this."

She straightens suddenly and laughs outright, slapping her thigh, pounding the ground with her cane, as though the body of the general were lying in front of her and she, gleefully, were stomping on it.

"And do you know what, *kind?*" She pokes me. "Do you know what? It was from that day, it was from that day that those Japanese were afraid of me. It was from that day they had respect and fear for me.

"So!" She stretches her arms out.

"Great!" I whistle back. We turn in our chairs, as if getting loose of them and each other.

"We should go inside now, Marget, hey? The sun is going down. Fan will be making dinner. All the good Indonesia food. Nasi goreng, and babi ketjap. And Fan's hot sambal. Delicious!" She grips my shoulder, helping herself up.

Later I watch her as she watches television. I sit in the darkness waiting for her tiniest, slightest flicker. Waiting for the moment she will betray herself, as I have. Her eyes follow the bright screen intently, her face a mirror of its yellows and greens. A country music star is on, singing about her cheatin' man. Gerda's face remains expressionless. The country star changes into a low-cut gown. Gerda remains unmoved. Beside her Fanny drops slowly off to sleep, her small head nodding down, the bole of a broken reed. Outside a car makes the slow round of my grandmothers' cul-de-sac.

My grandmother's cheek falls onto Gerda's shoulder. I notice how soft her mouth looks in sleep: moist, puckered, like a baby's.

"Ja." Gerda turns her head, seeing my look. "She's always like this, at night. She can never keep up with me."

"I'm sorry, Gerda." I always feel I have to apologize for the weakness of my blood. "I guess she's not as strong as you are." Then: "She never was, was she?"

"Strong? Oh, no! No. She is getting old. The doctor is saying it is her heart. He gives her little pills now for under her tongue. And also some other, to keep her from getting dizzy. Twice already this week she has had to take them. And then always at night, like this. Ah!" Gerda says, not moving Fan from her shoulder. "It can get lonely for me sometimes, you know."

Just before eleven o'clock, Gerda finally nudges her. "Fan! Hey you! Wake up! It's time to go to bed now."

My grandmother sits up, blinking.

"Would you like to stay down here for a while, Marget?"

"Can I?"

"Sure. You stay here, then. Only later you can turn off the lights over the kitchen sink. Also you can lock the doors."

"I will. Good night."

"Good night." She puts her hand on my shoulder. "*Wel te rusten.*"

"Good night, Oma."

"Good night, Marget," Fanny smiles, whispering, taking my face into her palms and laying her soft, perfumed cheek next to mine.

34

I come up after them to lock the front door. Gerda is already climbing the stairs. She is moaning, groaning softly in the night, crawling like an animal on her hands and knees, hissing from the pain. She winces and pulls herself up slowly, numbly, from step to step, while Fan hovers patiently behind, carrying Gerda's cane between her fingers like a black wand. Occasionally one of my grandmother's thin white hands rests like a petal on Gerda's hips. But if it's to steady one of them or both, I can't tell.

❧ Chapter Four ❧

There is the legend, in my family, that Oma Fan has special powers. That she can see and hear and touch things the rest of us can't see, hear, or touch. My father calls it Indonesian hogwash. My father is a businessman; he doesn't believe in the old voodoo, the ghost tales and spirit songs and demon stories, like the one Gerda loved to make me listen to when I was small, about the woman who looked beautiful but was crossed with a terrible scar.

This woman came out by moonlight, Gerda said, and could be recognized by the gleam on her long black hair. She would come to your well to wash herself, where she would bend and let her hair fall forward like a veil to hide her face. (Here Gerda would stop and imitate the demon, bending and folding her hair between her knees). But as soon as the demon did this, you could see what was so terrible and hideous about her. Because the hair hid a great gaping hole in her back, so deep you could look right through her.

Gerda said her sisters had run screaming whenever their *babu* told that tale. But fifty years later I just sat there, frozen, trying to look brave. Inside I was quivering like Jell-O. You don't forgive nightmares like that easily.

Unfortunately my grandmother's powers could no longer be demonstrated. Supposedly everyone knew they were real. My mother believed in them, though she acted around my father like she didn't. Gerda believed in them. Tante Pippy believed in them. But what can Oma Fan *do?* I asked my old aunt, when she came down from Reno to visit us.

Tante Pippy is Gerda's younger sister, and so also no relation to me. She is the most Indo-looking of them all, with bark-colored skin and almond eyes, and a firm, round body that makes her look like an old idol sitting in a chair. She lives in Nevada to be near the gambling—she can't live a life without risks, she told me, the war in the Indies made her too much used to it. She had looked down at my childish face kindly.

Why, she said, your grandmother can *move* things.

Move them? I said.

Sure, said Pip. Fanny moves things with her mind.

Oh, ja, she went on, Fanny had moved all kinds of things when she was younger. Card tables, and glasses on top of the card tables, and even cards placed on top of the glasses. Whiff! they blew away, just like a breeze had come under the door. Fan must have had a special mother, Pip said, because it runs only on the woman's side of the family. Look at me, Pip said, can I do such a thing? No! Look at Gerda. Could she guess all her Christmas presents before they were opened? No! "But your mama," Pip said, "she always can. She has her own way of knowing things, doesn't she?"

Once, as a test, I stole Mama's engagement ring and dropped it on the living room carpet. She found it the next day. She said afterwards she knew something was up, she'd had a strong urge to vacuum that morning.

"And don't you," Tante Pip asked me, "don't *you* ever feel the special power, sometimes? Don't you ever dream a thing, and then it happens? Maybe you think of something, just as the other person is saying it? Don't you ever jump, you notice, right *before* you hear a loud sound?" She looked closely at me, as if I were some kind of safe without a combination.

I thought maybe I had.

"Well," Tante Pip said. "Time will show. I tell you, it runs in your family, on the mother's side. I could never do a thing like that, no. Gerda could never do a thing like that. But you. You will be one of those who sees things." I ran that very morning out onto Gerda's back porch, to see if I could move things with my mind.

I saw, quite clearly, as if I'd never seen them before, the green stitches of porch screen, embroidered with columns of dew. I saw again, but with new, sharp eyes, the curve of the peacock chairs, the intricacy of their woven backs. I began staring, concentrated, at the asparagus fern, hanging loose and almost weightless in the muggy air. I chose one medium-sized spear, and focused all the energy of my nine-year-old brain on it, not blinking, until the tip wobbled from the tears swimming in my eyes.

I came inside after that, angry, disappointed, ashamed —because of course I must be some kind of sissy, if I couldn't even do what my old grandmother could. But I didn't dare ask Fanny to show me how.

"*Why?*" I asked Tante Pip, leaning once again on her hip. "Why doesn't Oma Fan do it anymore? Why won't she ever try to move things for us?"

"Because!" Tante Pip had said, lowering her double chin seriously and patting my waist. "Because! She is afraid of it!"

And that had made it all the more mysterious.

Because how could you call it a power, I wondered, if you were always too frightened to show it?

❧ Chapter Five ❧

In the morning it's the first thing I think about. Small, inescapable, hard, bruising, as painful as that princess's pea under twelve plump, downy feather mattresses. I am seven weeks pregnant. I knew, right away, after one missed period. The doctor at the women's clinic was careful to be neither happy nor sad for me. I guess they've learned, by now, how to make their faces neutral, a pull-shade hiding any revealing light. Soon after, I started waking up so sick in the mornings that I thought I could hear noises, crying, climbing like a tuning orchestra. And then I began to wonder: How do you know, really, what's objecting? Is it your body? Or your still unpregnant mind?

I have to be careful in the bathroom because Gerda and Fanny are awake and downstairs, and Fanny can be sensitive to sounds in the house. She might hear how

many times I've already flushed the toilet, might notice
and get suspicious, begin drawing the wrong conclu-
sions, thinking it was something she cooked for me. It's
true that I'm scalded on the inside, hugging the porce-
lain. I hate being in this position. I can't move, I might
fall. I have to wait until the roaring in my head subsides
and my breathing is even again.

When I come downstairs Fanny is inside her pantry.
She is moving things. Boxes of corn flakes and cans of
condensed milk, poring over them like an archaeologist
trying to sort the pieces of a ruined mosaic. She hates
that we have to eat and in this way destroy all her hand-
iwork. She shuffles and picks out and stores items
label-front again, frowning, clucking, discontented.

In the old house, Fanny's pantry had been as big as
some of the bedrooms. Gerda had added it next to the
kitchen, a kind of lean-to room with doors at both ends,
one to the kitchen, one going outside; the walls in between were lined with metal shelves secured with shiny
nuts bored like silver beetles into the paneling. Fanny
kept her shelves filled, no matter what the season. No
matter how much or how little we ate, or if it were the
Russians or Cubans coming one day. She kept endless
rows of dusty cans and mothy jars, bottles of dish soap,
packages of rice, canisters of oil, pickles, preserves, tins
of exotic spices, jugs of water. And hanging over it all,
as if it were really too much, too dangerous to leave exposed, long white curtains Fanny had made out of
sheets. They made the room look like a sleeping car on
an old train. I used to run between those sheets as if
something were hidden behind them, something that

might reach out and grab me. Something I wasn't supposed to know about.

Now, in this much smaller house, in the tiny pantry in one corner of the kitchen, without her sheets, my grandmother still hoards and packs.

Gerda is outside, washing her roses. She's squatting like a milkmaid on her stool, a heavy metal bucket between her knees filled to brimming with soap and water, and, with a sponge, is busy washing each green leaf, one by one. Soon the whole row will be gleaming and clean and waxy. This, Gerda once told me, is the only real thing to keep the spot away.

It's almost thirteen years since Gerda sold the old house to buy this new one. What seemed like a good idea at the time is now old in its turn, shabby, mildewy, run-down. I wonder if Gerda has ever had second thoughts. I wonder if she ever thinks she's made a mistake. Since she moved them they've never once been back to look at the old place. Gerda would never let on if she misses it.

In her pantry my grandmother clicks her tongue impatiently. I tap her shoulder from behind.

"Oma!" I point theatrically. "What's all this stuff in here?"

She giggles, shrinking like a fern from my touch.

"*Nee*, this is nothing." She blushes. "I used to have so much more."

She backs with an obeisance out of the pantry and into the kitchen. My grandmother's face and neck are powdered white, made up with her usual care. Her pink flowered blouse reaches to just above her angular, bookish hips; her pants are a soft blushing color to match; so are her pearl earrings and the pink of her frosted lipstick. My grandmother has always taken care with her appearance, has always made it clear, always reminded us, that she was a beauty—a face to be reckoned with. At Christmas she still makes her entrance at the bottom of the stairs in a shimmering green gown so eaten with age its fibers have begun to fall away from it, like hair. By the end of the evening she's left a trail of pale glitter, which my mother, in one of her own mismatched pantsuits, sweeps embarrassed into a waiting dustpan.

Fanny pushes me toward the kitchen table. It's time to eat. Gerda comes in, rubbing her chapped hands. She sits at the head of the table, leaning her cane against her chair.

"I'm *hungry*," she announces.

Fanny has set out slices of ham and cheese on a Delft blue plate. Also a plump loaf of white bread, with butter and jam, and a jar of Dutch spreading chocolate. So much sweetness makes my stomach jump into my mouth. Gerda looks over all the food and sighs, putting her hands with an effort under the table.

She is, she told me last night, on a "reducing plan" before her surgery.

"Eat!" she groans.

"Why don't you tell me more about this doctor of yours?" I'm trying to cheer her up. "You say he's a specialist, right?"

"Ja. An orthopedic surgeon. I can trust a man like that, Marget. He's real good. He says he is going to cut the arthritis out of my bone, and then make for me a

43

new knee. He will use metal screws, this big." She measures two inches beside her plate.

"You told him about your tennis?"

"He says I'm paying for that now. I said to him, 'Bah,
all the money is going to *you*.' But he is good. An Indian
—but very nice. He does this because I need it. You see
this powder in my glass? This is my special shake that I
take every morning for my breakfast."

She adds water from a measuring cup. She stirs it,
looks in at the color, sets her spoon aside, smells the
vanilla foam, takes a short sip, grimaces, and puts the
glass back on the table.

"Bah!" she says. "It's good, but it's not *so* good. Will
you pass me a little bit of the *brood* there, Marget? And
some chocolate. And maybe some *kaas*."

Fanny hands the plate with the sliced cheeses over.
She hardly touches any of the food herself, preferring to
eat all day, in tiny bites, like a bird. This is the Indonesian way.

My grandmothers are watching me elaborately chew-
ing my plain slice of bread.

"Eat more, eat more!" Fanny frowns.

"So Marget," Gerda interrupts. "How did you sleep
last night?"

"I've got some kind of backache this morning. Must
be from the flight over."

My grandmothers stiffen, offended. Then relax, re-
suming their meal.

"Oh, ja." Gerda nods. "That's okay, because you had
the long trip, and so on. But now, I don't understand

what you will do here, to keep busy. What, Marget, do you have planned for yourself?"

"Nothing. I'm just going to take it easy. Like a vacation. Relax."

"Ridiculous," she says, her mouth full. "You're too young to relax."

"I'll just have to find something to do, then. Is there anything you two need? Maybe I could do some dusting. I could get those cobwebs up there, in the corners. Or maybe I could go out on your driveway, Gerda, how about that, and wash your car. Or maybe I could do the yard. I could weed all the——"

"Stop!"

Gerda is scowling. Fanny is looking up, embarrassed, at the kitchen ceiling. It's as if I've caught them with their slips showing.

"What are you talking about?" Gerda frowns. "We don't need you to be doing things like that! We don't need to have any work done for us! Crazy. You go out now and you go shopping, you call your friends or you go to the movies."

"I don't have friends here anymore, Gerda. You know that. Anyway, don't you think we should spend some time together?"

"Hmph." She shakes her head. "You think we are going to die soon?"

"Vent!" my grandmother wails.

Tante Pip is wrong, of course. Gerda does see things.

"Of course not," I say.

But yes. It is exactly that, Gerda. It is exactly that I

think you are going to die soon. And I'm not sure if there's anything more I need from you.

"Maybe I should learn more about you. You know," I say casually, "for my children."

Gerda laughs, pointing her slathered buttered knife at me.

"Ja? Since when are you having children?"

"Someday."

"Oh, you mean for the future. Well. But what is the future? You tell me that, *kind*. There are so many kinds of future, and how do you know what will one day happen to you? What do you know about children, anyway? You, who don't even have a husband!"

"I don't—"

"What happened to that boy, that dancer boy you liked so much? You wrote us a letter about him, you remember that? Didn't you like to marry him, Marget?"

"He went to Europe. You wouldn't have liked him anyway. He was lazy. Don't look that way, Oma. We're not fighting."

But Fanny is trembling. She dreads an argument like a smoldering volcano. She winces as though our words are cinders flying charred around her.

"Look," Gerda says, seeing her face. "I don't mind you staying with us. You know that! We even *like* to have you with us. But I think, if you want to know something, you have to tell us something about *your* life. Anyway," she says easily, "maybe you'll never have children. Look at me. I didn't."

We sit silently for a moment, and Fanny lays one of her hands flat on the table, as if to hold it down.

"Yes, Gerda. But you have Corinne."

"Yes, but it's not the same."

"Anyway, I might have children. I just haven't decided yet."

"Hmph! You have to be married first."

"Not anymore."

"It's not right."

"It's modern times."

"Bah! Don't tell me about the time!" She sits straight up in her chair, as if I've stung her. "I *am* the time, Marget. I've seen all of this century, I tell you! Everything! I've been keeping up with it, running, the whole way. So you can't tell *me* what day is on the calendar. Nineteen-hundred and eighty-five. You can't tell me on what day I was born."

"Yes, Gerda, fine." My head is starting to throb. Maybe I should have eaten something more. Gerda's face is starting to float in front of me like a blimp launched off its cables. "I only meant that times have changed, Gerda. Since you were young. People have choices now. They can do whatever they want." I stress whatever. "They don't have to be afraid." Technically.

"You are naive, Marget! What do you know about afraid? You, little spoiled American girl! Twenty-two years old!"

"I thought you said it was a good age."

"Look, *kind*, I know things. I've been around for a long time. And I'm telling you: it is better to have a father."

All right, then:

"I wonder my mama didn't have one."

Everything stops. Their faces close to me as suddenly as shells. The kitchen is so quiet we can hear the ants scuttling on the windowsill.

Maybe I should just go lie down again. Just get up and leave them. But my head hurts, and my stomach. I can't move. I have to fight a heaving, rising, filling in the well of my throat.

I don't know how far we can go, if we're not going to talk about what we eat or how we slept. If we're ever going to talk about, admit, anything at all.

"But that's different." Gerda blinks, the first of us to recover. "That was special. A special case. And anyway," she breathes deeply, looking sideways at me, leaning back, "it's good to be married. Look at me. *I* was married." And she nods, wiping her forehead with her folded, embossed paper napkin.

But I can't stop myself. "So why didn't you have any children, then, before Rollie died?"

Fanny ducks as Gerda's napkin flies off the table.

"Why? Why?" She is shaking now. "Because! He was sick, if you like to know it! Sick! *Sick!* He had the tuberculosis, and you can't have any children with that! No, no, the doctor said no contact, no kissing, no touching, no nothing, never could we ever do anything like that, I could never even use the same spoon with him at the dinner table!"

"But that was all after you were married."

"No. Already before."

"Before?" I have to say it now, I can't help it, I have to push it, to force it out, because this is the first time we've ever gotten close to meaning anything. "Then you knew he was sick, before you married him. You knew it would never be like between a normal husband and wife. You knew you would never really be together, never have children, never have sex——"

Fanny blushes.

"Of course," Gerda says stiffly. "Rollie would not have lied to me."

There!

But when I look around, nothing has changed. We all sit in the same places. Nothing has moved.

"Bah!" Gerda sits regally back, waving her hand dismissively as if she gave me more credit than I deserved. "You don't know anything about the world, Marget. If you would have just known my Rollie. My boy. Then you would not have had so many questions. Then, you would understand. He was such a good man. So beautiful. Did you know that? So talented. And smart. And graceful, too. He could dance," she points to me, "like a Nijinsky, and all the girls in the nightclubs would want to go out with him. He could do anything he wanted, you see, because he was so beautiful, and an expert at so many things. He was what you would call today a real Renaissance man." She rolls the word off her tongue.

"You know the pictures there, in the living room?"

I nod, tired.

"He made them. He was a very sensitive man, my Rollie. Very gentle. He could look at a thing, and then he could copy it exactly, as though it came—how can I explain it?—blooming out of his brush. He could do

49

landscapes, which were always in ink, or in watercolors.
That is like what you see in there, that he made during
his grand tour of Europe. All the wealthy Dutch boys
were sent back, you see, to finish their educations. But
later, when he painted again in the Indies, his interest
became the female body. He was a specialist," she says
seriously, "of the breast."

"Nice!"

Gerda follows my pointed finger, looking down, surprised, at her two hands cupped on her blouse in front
of her. "Oh sure," she shrugs, unembarrassed. "He was
a good man with the breast, my Rollie. He was very—
observant. Let me tell you how he took me out with him
at night to hunt for prostitutes. Yes! He would tell his
driver where to take us, out into the *kampongs* where the
poorest of those kind lived. Oh, terrible places, by the
canals, and everything smelling of dung."

She curls her nose at my grandmother, who nods
silently. Gerda and Fan are fastidious. In Indies fashion,
they still keep a bottle of fresh water, always full, beside
their toilets, to rinse themselves with. But Gerda is poking me to keep my attention.

"Most of the women down there were Malay, and
they were terribly, terribly poor. They will do anything
you ask of them. Anything. And so Rollie, he would
make his driver go slowly, very slowly, just choosing, and
then, when he saw one in an alley that he liked—
poof!—I had to go down underneath his legs. Because
the girls didn't like to come forward if they saw there
was another woman in the car. And then Rollie would

call to his girl, and talk to her through the window, and make an arrangement with her. He would give her his card, and show her directions to his studio. I don't think they always believed him. They thought something more was going to happen. And then, when everything was finished and settled, and we are backing away from the alley, I can get up from the floor and look out the window and say what it is I think of her. Usually they are very skinny, these prostitutes Rollie likes. Like swans. With very long necks."

"But—didn't Rollie ever paint you, Gerda?"

"Me? Oh, no! He called me Dik, that was my nickname. It means fat. 'Dik,' he would say to me, 'what do you say we take the car to Bali this weekend?' Or, 'What do you say we go up into the mountains?' We were always having fun together, even when he was sick. Of course we were also very serious. My husband was an *artist*. His family, they wanted him to be an architect, like his father. *Toch*, my poor boy! His family were all very rich, and very old, and very stupid. They were one of the first Dutch barons in the colonies, you see, from the days of the spice companies, hundreds of years ago. So they think they are something special. Here is their crest."

She shows me her big signet ring, a golden griffin clutching an oar in its claws. "They would like to think they are still pure Dutch, these people, with no Indonesian in them. Ha! It was impossible. Rollie, he was blond, sure, like in his picture, but his mother and sister were the color of nuts, and they had black hair and black eyes, both of them, like me. But when Rollie wanted to marry me, hoo! there was such a fight, because of course I am mixed blood, and his parents are calling me an Indo, and saying that the only reason an Indo like me could ever meet a nice boy like him was because of my tennis playing—which was true, even though I couldn't play in the clubs for whites. Lucky for me my boy didn't listen to his family. He said he was going to marry me, and build us a beautiful house in the Jalan Margaguna. And he did it, you know—he designed it, and all of the furniture inside, and it was such a house, it was almost like music, you can't imagine. Wait, wait," she says excitedly, planting her cane. "I want you to see."

It would be nice to say something to Fanny, to talk to her. But the minute Gerda is gone Fanny is slipping off and away to some vague, empty train station she keeps inside her head. Where nothing, absolutely nothing, seems to be passing through.

I want to shout in one of her ears, What's going on? What are you thinking? Where are you now?

"Oma! Did you know Rollie?"

She blinks, coming back to me.

"Rollie?"

"Yes, Rollie. Did you know him?"

"Oh!" She begins to think, sitting up like a child in front of her teacher. "*Nee!* No. He died. Before I met Gerda. He died, Marget. It was a terrible thing." She clears her throat, already growing hoarse. "Gerda saw him die, in the hospital. He died of tuberculosis, Marget. Before the war."

She looks up at me. Calmly, as if Rollie's story can't touch her. She squints at me, as if looking for a flaw. Then smiles.

"Here!" Gerda says, breathless, returning from the living room. "Look." She pushes an old album in front of me.

The cover of it is faded leather, so dry at the corners that it has chipped, like wood. The black paper inside gives off an unfamiliar, musky odor, but also something familiar, some kind of memory—a mixed smell of skin and earth and wood and smoke, perhaps. Now I remember. I know these pictures. I've seen them before. The glue at their edges has turned crystalline, falling out like the wings of dead insects.

"Here," Gerda says, "here is where we lived."

We look inside.

Here, she points, is the library. Here is the salon, with the piano. See here, how he made the chairs, echoing the instrument, curving also along with the stairs. Here is the terrace, here is my boy's studio, and here is an unfinished oil painting, called *The Three Graces.*

I look, leaning in. The graces are blond and thin and drooping; they have bobbed, marcelled hair. Little cherry-pursed mouths. Just like chorus girls.

"Rollie built me this house, Marget, even though he knew he would not live in it for very long. He finished it just before the war, just before he died."

So that's why everything looks so fresh, so untouched. "How did you keep these pictures?"

"In a tool box, during the war. I buried them. And I took some of Rollie's drawings too, the ones you see in the living room, and I rolled them up and I hid them inside the canisters for tennis balls. I buried them in the yard, also. I buried our money there too. Silver. We lived off that, after the occupation. But later we had to leave everything. And then, when we were gone, the Indonesians dug everything up. They were like animals, Marget, they threw all of this away. They think it means nothing. But I had an old Chinese friend. He found these in the trash near my house. He sent them to me in Holland."

"Do you remember?" I turn to Fan, trying to draw her in with us.

"Oh yes." She nods dreamily. "I lived there. After Gerda found me in the street."

"No, Oma. You mean after you met in a bomb shelter."

"What? No!" Gerda waves her hand impatiently. "Who told you that? Your mama? She is always making things up, when she doesn't know what she is talking about. No. I met Fan during the classification."

"What's that?"

But now Fanny, surprising, jumps in. "*Toch!*" she says. "That is when they try to decide what you are."

They were forced, all the citizens of the port city of Surabaya, to come out of their houses and stand in long lines in the hot, tree-lined streets. They were driven by the Japanese soldiers with their mounted bayonets toward intersections, where the officers waited, surrounded by armed guards, at long, official-looking tables. There you were asked for your papers. If you were Dutch, you were sent to the camps. If you were blond, you were sent to the camps. If you were pale-skinned, or your eyes were too light, or you forgot to look down, or you didn't look humble enough, you were sent to the camps. If you were male you were sent to the camps.

"Your grandfather!" Fan jumps in again. "You know how they already had taken him? You know about your grandfather, and how he was taken away into Burma?"

He told me something about it once in a letter. Something about a Railroad of Death.

"He was a nice man," Fan says dreamily.

"Shush!" Gerda says. "I am talking here! So. I am standing, in this line, with all these people, in the street. I have my sisters with me. Their husbands have already been taken to the camps, they were the first ones to go. So we are walking, very slowly, saying nothing. And then I see this little woman, here, in front of me. She is holding her little baby, like a doll. And that baby is cry-ing, and that woman is crying, and they are so scared, they are sick, they can't stop."

"I was so afraid of those Japanese," Fanny says.

"Then, when it comes her time to go up to the table, she can't move. She only stands there with her papers, opening her mouth, like this!" Gerda opens and closes her teeth, like a fish gasping.

"I had green eyes," Fanny says. "And blond hair."

"So you can see," Gerda nods matter-of-factly. "You can see, this one here, she is never going to make it. But then I say to myself: No! I cannot let this woman go. I cannot let these Japanese have her. I must think fast, and try to help her, and also that poor little baby. Because if I don't do something right away, Marget, then you are never born." She holds open her hand, showing how she once had the power of life and death over me.

"So! I walk right up to that table with her, and I stand right in front of that officer. I see he is about to send Fan to the camps. And I say, 'Wait! Wait! Please, most honorable sir! Please wait. This woman, let me explain, she is with me. This is the sister of my brother's wife, who is ill since the birth of her child. She cannot speak. It is so sad, she is such a good woman, and now we are giving a home to her. Look, sir, she will give you no trouble. She is Indonesian, like me. She is Indo. She only dyes her hair yellow to look like the movie stars. Please, sir, take all of our papers. We are all Indonesians here, you can see that, we are all Asian brothers together!'

"And then I push Fanny in with us, and Elly and Pip together, and everyone is so surprised we can say nothing. We just stand there. And the officer, he looks to see us better. Now I am sure we are *all* going to the prison camps. But then another woman, she comes forward, right toward us. A big Javanese, with all her little children. Five little children, I remember that, starting maybe from five years old. And this big Javanese woman, she shouts to the officer:

"'Wait, let me speak! Hear me, you! This woman is not Dutch, I tell you. She is not Indonesian. She is not Chinese. She is not British. She is a mother, like me!

Look at us! *Ik ben 'n moeder!'* She shouts it like this. Hitting her stomach. '*Ik ben 'n moeder! Ik ben 'n moeder!* So if you say this woman is Dutch, I am Dutch. All of us here! We all are Dutch!' And she lifted her big brown hands at him.

"I don't know why that woman spoke that way, for us. She is not anybody we know. But then, the next thing we see, they are taking her away. They took her, and all of her five little children, maybe from five years old, and they put them in the trucks. And they let us go. They forgot about us. I don't understand it, still. I don't understand why she shouted that way, for us." She stares at the table, my old not-grandmother, trying to see through the wood.

"And then," Fanny prods me, "Gerda took me to her house. I never see something so beautiful. I was always so poor!"

"Poor Oma!" I say, squeezing her hand to remind her it's no longer the case.

Gerda looks at us, pleased. There, you see? her narrowed eyes speak to me. You see how I had to take of her, this poor, defenseless little creature?

My eyes wander to the album again. Of course I know there's nothing in it that has anything to do with Fan. It's only Gerda and her large family, thick-browed, muscular, with smooth Indo faces under their black, marcelled hair. Gerda in her early twenties, showing off her tennis whites. Gerda surrounded by a group of boys, joking at one of the sports clubs. Gerda at the docks with her first car, a coupe; Gerda with her friends, getting ferried by long poles to Bali. Gerda's parents, good-looking, prosperous burghers, half Asian, half European in their cool, beaded dress. Sisters and brothers and uncles and aunts and cousins, all of them, all posed in front of a huge, tile-roofed house.

But there are no people left for Fanny. No family, no past. No hazily pictured beginnings. Even if I try to reach back like this, for the faces, a place—I find nothing.

I look again, staring hard at Gerda's people. I concentrate, I try. But I can't do it. I can't move them. I can't trace, in their faces, lines that are my own.

"Oma." I turn to Fan. "Was it so hard, living in the orphanage?"

"No, no," she reassures me, patting my hand. "They gave me dancing lessons."

✠ Chapter Six ✠

I can do it if I make an effort. I can tie together all the little facts I know about Fan's life into a small, hard knot about the size of a bean. It feels odd, like assembling a minute jigsaw you know will have crucial pieces missing. I don't know where to begin. I'm uncertain about things like order.

I think people should come with maps. Everyone should have her destiny stencilled clearly on the palm of her hand.

Of course Fanny could help me, a little bit. But she doesn't. She only shrugs when you try to ask about the past, as if to say, That's all done, that's nothing that matters now, to anyone, anymore. She sometimes hints that she was lonely, and lucky to have Gerda find her; then she retreats again into her vagueness, the masked safety of her lovely face. But why are you so *distant?* I want to ask her. Why are you so demure? What do you do when you've tiptoed onto the far edge of yourself and you find you're way too little to get by with, or worse, way too much?

She isn't like my mother, who churns out words like a paddlewheel. Mama, for the most part, likes to keep moving. It's her way of staying afloat, of not feeling the cramp.

My grandmother was the daughter of a French-Dutch father and a Javanese mother. This much I know. There were records from before the First World War, Gerda told me—birth certificates, marriage licenses, parish registries—but most of these were eventually lost through fires and wars and successive typhoons. There are other, simpler records, of course. I think my great-grandparents must have been an elegant couple. Fanny moves sometimes, inside her old bones, with an effort-lessness that can't be taught, with a wordlessness that sometimes murmurs. As if there were a kind of history written inside the body. She had a younger brother named Theo, like van Gogh's, and an older sister called only Zus. They lived in a house at the edge of a coffee plantation, although it isn't clear now if Fanny's father owned the land. These are only pale memories she passed along to Gerda, and that Gerda, like a spy, slipped across to me. Fanny no longer talks about them.

In 1919, when Fanny was four years old, the great in-fluenza epidemic came to Java. A guest of the house caught it, and gave it to my grandmother's family. Zus was the first one to die. They didn't have time to place a gravestone. Fanny's mother became ill, and was finished within a week. Uncles died, and cousins, and neighbors; servants locked the doors leading in and out of all the bedrooms, not wanting to go near the demon slithering through the house, not wanting to let it loose to ravage their *kampongs*.

One night when Fanny lay sweating with her fever barely broken, her *babu*, her nurse, came into her room. The old woman picked Fanny up and carried her under the armpits, down the stairs and through the garden and away from the blazing house. Its lanterns had all been lit to mourn the death of my great-grandmother. Outside, the other servants were crouching, hiding behind some bushes. They had Theo, and kept his baby's mouth covered. In the stables Fanny could hear her father shooting the horses, one by one. She could hear him, working methodically, and the huge bodies of the animals falling like trees to the dust.

The next day Fanny's father shot himself in the head in his wife's bedroom. He was standing over her body, and when he fell across her a black liquid oozed from her mouth. The servants took the children quickly away from the house to the *kampong*, until Fanny and Theo were stronger and it was believed the black demon had passed. Not knowing what else to do with them, the servants took the children to the colonial officials. Fanny and Theo no longer had surviving relatives, so each was sent to a home for foundlings.

My grandmother never saw her brother again. He was sent to a home for boys, she to a home for girls. My great-grandparents' estate was probably sold to pay off debts, and their children weren't given so much as a locket. Perhaps everyone thought it was better.

At the orphanage my grandmother was kept by Portuguese nuns. At first they told her they would have to shave her head. My grandmother whimpered and tried to hide in a nun's skirts. It isn't going to hurt her, one said; we have to make certain she doesn't carry lice, said another. Perhaps something was added here, between the darker, older women; perhaps that Fanny's hair, like the Virgin's, was too beautifully golden to shear. Because in the end my grandmother had her hair bobbed, and got to keep the rest of it folded in a piece of white tissue. When they sent her out into the world, years later, she got to take the gift of her hair along with her, carrying it inside her purse like rolled money.

Fanny grew up in the orphanage. She was given lessons in embroidery and sewing, and learned reading and writing and music. A dancing master came to teach them balance, because gracefulness, he said, made for good servants and good wives. Fanny liked the dance lessons. She kept them up by herself for years afterwards. When she was eighteen the nuns let her go from their walls, giving her money and finding a room for her, and work in a beauty salon. There Fanny learned to wash and cut Dutch women's hair, and did manicures and pedicures, bathing their feet.

But at night, Gerda told me, Fanny loved to go out to the clubs. To the hot spots, where all the young Dutch kids went dancing and drinking, and where Fanny could pass for one of them with her pale, powdered good looks. I can see her, or almost see her, with her long, French-twisted hair, swaying in the arms of those bright Dutch boys, moving her lips to the jazz. But then a curtain falls; she's cut off from me. Not one image from the years of her marriage. When I see her again she is crying, facing the Japanese, and Gerda is shoving her family forward to save her.

❈ Chapter Seven ❖

At the end of our first week together it's time to dye Gerda's hair. Her roots are coiling like nests of steel wire over her forehead, making her look more fierce, even, than usual.

I sit at the kitchen table, watching. Fanny measures the bottle of dark chemicals absently, as if her hands have done the work far too often. She dabs at Gerda's scalp with the nozzle, massaging the color in with her curled, gloved fingers. When she's done she twines Gerda's head, turban-style, in Saran Wrap, until my other grandmother is lost under a glittering cocoon.

Gerda sits patiently for all of this on her stool in front of the kitchen sink, a towel protecting her neck. Fanny hovers around her in a flowery robe, her own hair spiked like a Jabberwock's.

When Gerda is finished Fanny dyes her own roots a deep magenta brown. Fanny stopped being a blond, Gerda told me, quite naturally in middle age. While they wait for their colors to set they trade places and Gerda begins massaging Fan's neck. Her touch is mechanical, a matter of habit. As if she were simply buffing up a tarnished tray.

"Here now, you do it, *kind*. She likes it hard."

I feel funny, running my hands along my grandmother's papery skin. The muscles around her neck are surprisingly stiff.

"No, harder," Fanny complains. "It's not enough."

But my wrists are already aching from tugging at her. If I pull any harder, I think, I will tear you right off the bone.

"*Nee*, no, let Gerda do it," she says finally. "You don't know how to do it like your mama can."

"I don't want to hurt you."

"*Nee*. You can't hurt me."

Our day has settled into a simple routine. In the morning we have our Dutch breakfast, along with Gerda's half-touched glass of diet powder. Afterwards Gerda and I sit sunbathing in the yard, or weeding the flower beds; Fanny stays inside with her pantry or her laundry, or wipes her tarnished candlesticks, the leaves of her indoor plants. After lunch Gerda likes to drive, slowly, five blocks to the grocery store, to buy whatever fruits were on sale in the morning paper. Fanny stays home, waving at us, refusing to budge from the porch.

After dinner they watch television while I play solitaire on the carpet, until Fanny drops off to sleep, falling like a weighted scale at Gerda's side.

I'm eight weeks pregnant now. Nothing shows. And yet I know it's right there, trying to get ahead of me, in front of me, before I'm ready; I can feel it gathering force, building like a wave underneath a prow. It's three days now until the surgery. Fan shivers whenever she hears the word "operation," her head shrinking like a lily between her shoulders.

I've called the doctor, or rather the nurse, to find out what I should expect. She told me it was all fairly routine and said I should relax. They would do only one knee this time, the left, because it was the stronger, and would make for easier recovery and rehabilitation. You don't have to worry, she told me. Your grandmother's a bit old for the procedure, but perfectly fine, and her heart is as strong as an ox's. She'll be leaping around again like a woman of sixty. There will be therapy to help her along.

I try to impress all of this on Fanny while she sits over her morning coffee cup, ready to disappear into her void.

"But I don't like it." She shivers. "It doesn't feel right. I feel something will go wrong, this time."

"Look!" I nudge her, pointing at my feet, kicking off one of my slippers.

Her eyes grow wide.

"Oooh. So *ugly*."

"See? We're tough."

My grandmother has always taken a peculiar kind of pride in my callused feet. "How hard you are working.

66

So much?" She stares fascinated at my toes the way some people look at bullfights. We both stare at them. Above the smooth linoleum of the kitchen floor they look something like chunks of granite: pink, with bluish bruises, and rosettes of still-red blisters. My toenails are thick and look like unpolished quartz. (How long will it take, I wonder, for my feet to look normal again?)

"Watch this."

I get up and step out of the kitchen and lie back on the living room carpet. She can see me from where she sits. I pull my right leg in my sweatpants back to my left ear, then do the same thing with my left leg, stretching it back to my right.

"Oooh!" My grandmother's eyes focus with delight. She likes limbos and contortions, all things strange and circus-like. She's impressed, and distracted from her worry—which makes me feel a little less guilty for giving her this false impression. I can't bring myself to tell them. I don't know how many bombs I can safely drop.

I've never once seen Fan gesture to the old, balletic movements she must still, certainly, know. She is graceful, she is balanced, she sometimes moves like a swan across a deep pond. Yet why doesn't she arch her foot, curve her arm, or stretch her neck out along a remembered angle? Antique motions can be truly comforting. My own stretches are burning at predictable degrees down my thighs. I am like a harp, and I'm playing a familiar tune across myself. Some contortions you practice so long they begin to feel natural.

The kitchen telephone rings. I jump up to get it.

"Marget, hon! Is everything okay?"

It's Mama, shouting, breaking up—the echo of her voice chasing itself across the Atlantic. "How are you? Are you getting along out there okay? Are they starting to drive you crazy? Are you getting enough to eat? Yes? Yes? Well, that's good." I can hardly get a word in. "I wanted to call and say hello and talk to Gerda just for one minute. To wish her luck, the crazy *ouwetje*, for her thing. I know you'll be keeping an eye on Fan, especially while Gerda's out. You might try to get Gerda to say something about her will. If you can. Just to make sure she has everything in order. I suppose Fan's all the time trying to stuff you with food?"

I don't say anything, hoping she'll notice the silence.

"I guess there's not really much for you to do out there, is there? I'm sorry, hon. But we sure do appreciate this. Are you getting some good workouts out there? Oh that's good, that's good. You always have to worry about getting out of shape." Her voice has grown puzzled, amazed, as it does whenever she mentions my dancing. "But just be careful. Don't stress yourself out. Take it easy. Give yourself a nice rest. Well, I guess you'd better let me talk to Fan and Gerda now, before this gets too expensive. Take care of yourself, now. We love you. Bye-bye." I unwind the phone cord, reluctantly, from around my finger.

My grandmothers' faces brighten as each pushes her ear up to the receiver, sharing it. They scold, and pout, and plead with my mother. "What? Why for so long? What are you doing? Why can't you come home? Where are you going? When are you leaving? What are you doing now?" She doesn't give them time, either, to get in the right words. It's a good trick, Mama's. Like fencing without the blood.

"I can't understand it." Gerda scowls as she hangs up. "Always she is staying away from us. Always she is running, and running."

I sit playing solitaire, after dinner. My grandmothers, with the strange, supple memory of very old people, have all but forgotten my mother and her neglect. They even seem peaceful. They sit a little apart on the Danish loveseat in front of the television. Gerda has a sportscast on. Fanny is watching too, her eyebrows arching a bit, as if she's receiving information she can't quite decipher.

We start at a sharp knock at the door.

"You get that, Marget. It's the Boy Scouts."

I can hear Gerda's voice rising behind me as I start down the hall. "Fan!" she cries. "Ha! Did you see that? Did you see that one? That ace? Ha! How the other one couldn't even try to return it!" The words float over me as I open the door.

"Marget!"

"Corinne!"

My aunt stands under the porch light, insects dancing mazy above her head. She exhales and a long blue stream of cigarette smoke fills in the porch between us.

"Well, hey!"

"Hey, you!"

We're laughing and hugging and poking each other in the ribs all at once. Corinne takes another drag from her cigarette and blows it like a kiss next to my ear.

Then she pulls back from me, her right wrist jangling, full of bangles. She is squinting, judging my looks. Tiny lines are starting, like spiders' legs, around her eyes. Corinne must be thirty-seven now.

She comes in with her clouds of smoke and her heavy, expensive-smelling perfume. Corinne, whom I also call my tante, is Gerda's adopted daughter, and also no blood relation to me. She is Gerda's niece, the child of one of Gerda's brothers who died in Holland after the war. She was wild as a little girl, my mother used to tell me, wild for having been raised without a mother, wild for having only a young-old war-broken father, who did nothing but pine for his dead wife in his tiny Dutch government—owned house. Gerda took Corinne when she was six years old. Mama had just turned fifteen. From what I can tell, they mistrusted each other on the spot.

Soon after, Gerda put everyone on a boat for America. By then she had waited nearly ten years to get permission to emigrate. Only in America, Gerda believed, would she have the old freedom again. Only in America could she start her life over, and have something again like her old, comfortable ways. She never liked Holland, she told me, she didn't know anything about it—even though it was part of her blood. She was Indonesian, she was a colonist, she knew nothing about the Old World. So she sold her narrow three-story Rotterdam house, and took what was left of the family by then—Fan, Pip, Elly, my mother, and Corinne—to see the New World, and begin fresh. Gerda was fifty years old.

"Are they in there?" Corinne asks, slipping sideways into the kitchen to crush her cigarette out in the sink. "Are they sleeping on the sofa, those lazy *ouwetjes?*"

America agreed with my aunt's wild ways. Gerda tried beating her into good behavior, but it didn't work. Fan tried coaxing and candy and scolding. Corinne didn't listen any better in the new country than she did in the old one. She swore in English, and played with the boys in the streets, and stole candy from Woolworth's and tore the new dresses the Foreigners' Aid Society kept giving them. I remember years later, when we got together for Christmas dinners at the old house, how Gerda would find a moment, always, to lecture Corinne about her childhood, right in front of all of us. She acted as if Corinne weren't even there, or as if she were only temporarily in the room, like the fake holly and the lights and the plastic, plugged-in Santa Claus.

"Ja," Gerda would say, pointing at my mother. "Our little Frances here, she was a wonderful child. She did everything we told her to do, she studied hard in school, she went to her dancing classes, and then she, she——" here Gerda would get a little stuck——"she married a nice young man." Gerda bowed, a little angrily, across the table to my father. "But now, Corinne—no! No. She did nothing, never, for anyone. She was a terrible, horrible little girl."

Corinne would wink at me and say nothing, half-smiling, half-staring down at the flocked tablecloth. Yet she was the one who came and stayed with my grandmothers during Elly's last, long, terrible illness. She was the one who always remembered the *ouwetjes* when my parents began to forget, writing them letters, bringing them presents, visiting and reading out loud to them from *Reader's Digest* and *The Indo*. She brought flower seeds they saved in their packages and never planted, she changed their light bulbs and called the plumber when their water faucets dripped at night like pure torture.

In return for this, Gerda pays Corinne's credit card bills, and settles her speeding and parking tickets. She writes a large check after every one of Corinne's divorces. Corinne so far has married three wild men in a row. The first turned out to be a drug addict. He hit her with a car muffler, and a year later she left him. The second had had polio when he was young and walked with a romantic, swaggering limp. He flew into rages whenever Corinne looked at other men, and finally punched a hole in the kitchen wall beside her head, so she left him. The last one seemed more serious and stable, even though he was a rock musician. Until one night he exploded in my grandmothers' living room, demanding money from Gerda, trying to throttle her. Fanny fainted, Corinne called the police, and number three disappeared, never to be seen again except in court papers.

Corinne would wander away for a time, to Mexico, Florida, Texas. But she always came back whenever her luck—or her money, as my father bluntly put it—ran out. But *why*, I've heard my mother scold Gerda many times, why do you always let her come back to you? Why can't she learn, why can't she make her own mistakes, without you always being there, ready to catch her? Why do you protect her so especially?

"Because," Gerda answered. "She is my blood." And that, every time, has put an end to it.

Now I watch Gerda and Corinne hug each other with a mixture of warmth and suspicion. They are like water and oil, these two women, coming together; it's hard to believe they share so much blood. Corinne is tall and shapely and feminine, she wears a tight leather mini-skirt, and her hair is cut in a bob, pert and shiny. Fan kisses her tenderly on the cheek, leaving a lip mark Corinne has to rub away, laughing. Gerda gestures to the furniture and we all sit down, carefully, as if poised on mushrooms.

"So," Gerda begins. "What are you doing here? You are coming about my surgery, too?"

"No—but Tante Pip told me about it. Why didn't you?" She lifts an arm and shakes out her bracelets. Gerda says nothing, *hmph*ing. "I'm on my way up to Reno. Pip knows I'm coming to see her. They're getting ready to hire some new people out there for this fancy new casino they're opening." She smiles, looking brightly around the room, at the walls, the pictures, the candlesticks rising from small to large like organ pipes on the fake mantel. They were her Mother's Day present to Fan and Gerda. She shakes back her hair. Corinne isn't beautiful, but she has made-up good looks. Hers is the organized, put-together face I see on flight attendants, and actresses, and waitresses.

"What about Los Angeles?" Gerda asks.

"Too much smog. I didn't like it."

"But the tips were good down there, you said."

"Yes. No. Not really. The tips weren't so good any-more, where I was working. People down there are like sharks—you know, they keep moving. It's hard to make money." She leaves a gap here. "Oh, wait!" she cries, digging into her purse. "Look what I got you!"

She pulls out two small, hastily wrapped packages.

"Corinne!" Fanny lights up. "You shouldn't! Always you are buying too much."

"No, no, it's okay, it's just from the tar pits. Things get stuck in there, from way back. I thought you might like them, the way the little twigs float inside." She turns and winks at me, as if I were a co-conspirator. But then we've always had something special between us. Some-thing simple, but true: Corinne and I are the youngest in our small family.

I watch her as she watches my grandmothers opening and exclaiming over and then quickly forgetting their charms. Corinne's eyes are the only thing about her that is like Gerda. They are sharp, and narrow, and watchful, and they seem to look out on a world that has to be shaken for whatever it can give you. But with Corinne there is something different—a look of anxious, hungry longing. As if she were hunting for a cushioned alley, a door opening onto a perfect, rainbow's end back lot.

The rest of her face is tanned and lean and unfamil-iar, the face of a long-dead woman, of her dead mother long gone and buried. You can't make Corinne any more like you, I think to Gerda. You never will. There is someone else in there, lost inside her, but still powerful, fighting you for her blood.

"I can only stay a little bit." Corinne fidgets. "I have to keep going tonight. Need to be there first thing in the morning. Got to look good for those managers. Say, Mama," she turns to Fan, "can I get some things out of your pantry? Just a few things, to get me started, you know."

"Of course, Corinne! You go, you go!"

"I'll come with you," I say.

"Good, we'll have a nice chat. Now you two," she says to my grandmothers, "you just sit right there and let us do all the work. Just stay, and be comfortable. I know you've got *Dynasty* coming on."

"So how are you doing, kid?"

Corinne jangles the light cord in the pantry, her long red nails jumping into the glare. "Turn around now, and let me get a good look at you. Ooh, you're picking up some weight! What are you blushing for? Come on, it's okay. You could use it. So what's that you have on under your sweatpants, some kind of leotard or something?" She looks me over again, the way she did at the front door. "Okay now, let me see your feet.

"Yuck! And a nice pretty girl like you, too. Don't you feel embarrassed when you have to go buy sandals? Now me," she says, turning her ankles out, "I got a pedicure last week. On Rodeo Drive." Her toes are red and recent, like her fingernails.

75

"So what do you think?" She pivots.

"You always look good, Tante. Mama would be so mad. And you saw how glad Fan was to see you. You're like a Christmas present, practically."

"I know, I know." She reaches for a brown paper bag on the bottom shelf. Serious wrinkles turn down like half-moons at the corners of her mouth. "But she looks so thin, Mag. Doesn't she? I mean—wasted. Do you think she's really okay? How's her blood pressure doing?"

I don't even know. How was I to know this was something I should ask about? "I think she's just worried about Gerda's surgery."

"Well, who wouldn't be? It's like arming a Russian tank or something. But Fan shouldn't get all nervous about it, Gerda'll be just fine. Mag, it's Fan I worry about."

Corinne is the only one who calls me by that ugly, witch-wonderful name that makes me feel like I could mix up a brew, soar over castles, turn people into pumpkins, salamanders. Corinne is loading up Cheese Nips, packing thoroughly, as if for a long climb. "I keep thinking she's going to fall down," she says. "Fan. One day on those stairs. Have you seen that routine? Gerda going up on her knees? Pip says it's been like that since last year, maybe longer. Why Gerda bought a tall house I'll never know. Just like Holland. Hand me another bag from down there, will you?

"I'll bet Fan isn't even taking her potassium. She was in there starting to have one of her spells, I could see it. Just completely blanking out on us."

"I thought she was just getting old."

"She's not that old, Maggie. She's barely seventy."

"I could tell how much she liked the amber."

"You really think so?" Corinne stops, looking pleased at me. "I really got those for Fanny, you know. She'll wear them. She needs them, in a way, to make her feel pretty. Of course, if I'd known you were here, I would've brought you some too. Say, it's still great in here, isn't it? Just like a food market. Nothing compared to the old house, though."

She pokes me. "Remember how I always used to go out and buy you stuff?"

Corinne was a generous aunt. She bought me bell-bottoms and halter tops when I was a kid, hoop earrings and tiger's-eye bracelets, and then once, a beautiful little pink silky negligee, wrapped in white tissue paper, for my twelfth birthday. Mama didn't like it. Too risqué. "I still have the belly chain you gave me, you remember?"

"Eighteen inches. Too big. And your mama didn't like me giving you gold. She said it cost too much, for a teenager. But you know, you always looked like you needed a little something to me. I mean, I never heard about you going out with boys, or on dates. Weren't you kind of lonely?"

"Not really." I thought I was better than other kids, because I knew already what I wanted to be.

"Well, probably you just didn't notice it. Anyhow," she says, "I had to be giving you things. Because you're like my niece."

She unfolds one more paper bag, flapping it out like clean laundry.

"So what are your parents doing these days?"

"Oh, you know them. Off. Making money."

"Must be nice. I hear your mom's got a real pretty house now, in London. Tante Pip sent me some pictures she sent her."

"They're thinking of buying a place in France now."

"Wow! No kidding. What a life. I would've thought that now that—No no no, we're fine, Mama, Gerda. Just stay there, stay put!" She hurries to fill the last bag with boxes of instant cereal. "Just like a couple of old hens. Help me carry this stuff to my car, okay? Or else Fan will come in and start complaining I've moved things around."

Corinne's car is a convertible. The kind of car she took me out in to see the salt flats when I was little, letting me sit on her knees and pretend I was driving, craning over the dash. She used to find me playing alone at Gerda's and Fan's, when she must have been between jobs and husbands, needing distraction, and thinking I needed—something.

This one is a fifteen-year-old Mustang.

"You know what," she says, slamming the trunk and leaning against it, feeling inside her pocket for her cigarettes. "I always knew your mama was going to end up a lucky married woman. I really did. I knew it the first time I saw your dad. Ten years old, I was. I knew she had this new date coming, see, so I went down the block to try and scare him."

She leans into the open car for her lighter, straightens up with her mouth in a pucker. "That," she exhales, "was back when we lived in the pink house. You didn't know that pink house, Marget. It was awful. It was when we first got to America. We were living in Oakland. Three tiny little rooms, and a tiny little kitchen, for all six of us. Yuck! But anyway, your mom, even then she managed to get all the best boyfriends around. I don't know how she did it. She wasn't pretty. Her English wasn't very good. I don't even know how far she let them go. Of course she was smart, and funny, and kind of different, so she really played on that. Not me—I always wanted to fit in. But I looked up to your mom, you know, for being so sharp about everything. I was just dumb in school myself. And your mother, she knew how to read books, and how to look good in dresses. You should have seen her in all those petticoats."

Corinne takes another pull on her cigarette, looking toward the house. It's strange, hearing my mother come dragging from her lips. I feel a sudden pang of envy that Corinne knew my mother when she was young.

"Anyway," she goes on, "so your mom's date I was looking for, I thought he was an American. Because I didn't know then your dad was English, about his parents coming here like us, all of that. And then I saw him. And wow, I mean, you should have known him then, he looked just like a movie star! He was really incredible looking, like Clark Gable or Cary Grant or something. And I went running back to the house shouting, 'There's a movie star coming down our street!

There's a movie star coming down our street!' And your mom, she just, you know, looked out the window real casual and said, 'Oh, no. That's just my date.'

"But that was your mom—none of the boys was really a big thing to her. She was always—I don't know, kind of distant. Like somehow they weren't what she was looking for. But pretty soon, all of a sudden, she got really excited about your dad. She always liked *Ivanhoe,* and then he was British and all of that. I remember one night, sitting up in bed waiting for her, late, and finally she came home, and she came in, and she sat down on our bed, and she said to me, 'Corinne, I'm going to marry that man.' Just like that. Like maybe she'd only just decided.

"Of course Gerda was mad as hell. Especially after she found out your mom was pregnant. Nobody ever wants to admit anybody does anything like *that,* not in this family. And your mom wasn't married yet. Plus Gerda just plain didn't like your dad—it drove her crazy how he wouldn't take any guff from her. Gerda only likes men she can control. They say that's how it was with Rollie. That he just did whatever she told him to. Just like a slave."

I don't know if I believe it. But Corinne flicks her cigarette ash, shrugging. A corner of my picture of Rollie begins to crumble. It might be true. Gerda might have lorded over him, too.

"But I mean it's obvious, isn't it? Just look what happened to me."

"Well, what happened?" Because Corinne always likes to imply it was Gerda who somehow ruined her marriages, that everything would have been fine except for her, no beatings, no car mufflers. But how Gerda could have been responsible for all that, it's hard to imagine.

"Oh, let's not get into it. Let's just go inside."

⊰ Chapter Eight ⊱

"Y**ou're sure you can't stay the night?" Gerda says as we come back into the house.

"Positive." Corinne leans against the living room sheers, looking through them, then looks around until her eyes light on the gleaming Javanese wall lizard. She goes over and rubs its back. "Think this will bring me luck?"

"Did you get enough from the pantry?"

"Ja, *bedankt*, Mama. I'm taking everything over to Tante's first. She's putting me up till I find my own place."

"Oh!" Fanny exclaims. "Pippy will like that."

Corinne grimaces at me. It isn't true. Tante Pip would much rather not be bothered by us. She would much, much rather keep away from all of us, something she's made quite clear by buying a condo five hours away on the other side of the Sierra Nevada. At first she and Elly had moved only two hours away, to a small apartment in Sacramento. Then Elly died and Pip struck out even further, like a pioneer, all the way out of the state. Marget, I don't mind being alone, she once told me. I've had too many years of living with *those* people. She jerked her head toward the surrounded Christmas table. She said she didn't even really miss her husband, although he had been a kind man. He had died of something called Happy Feet, in the prison camps. She said she hardly remembered him.

Tante Elly hardly remembered her husband, either. But then Tante Elly had hardly remembered anything —she'd been shell-shocked during the war. When I was small she had walked around the old house, tottering, as though her mind were still wearing its nightgown. But Pip said Tante Elly had been good company, in spite of her forgetfulness. She had been quiet, and neat, and always ready to go.

"Tell Pip then to come and see us," Gerda says.

"Well, I'm sure she'd like that."

"Well. If you are going tonight for such a long drive, then, you'd better sit down and have some coffee. Fan?"

Corinne hesitates, looking trapped. She drops into a chair. My grandmother glides on her invisible rails into the kitchen.

Gerda plants herself on the loveseat across from Corinne.

"So what have you and Marget been talking about? Hey? She has been here for a week, did she tell you?

Doing nothing. Just looking at us. I told her she thinks we are old and going to die soon."

"I wonder whatever gave her that idea?"

"She doesn't tell us." Gerda shrugs. "But at least she is right, to be thinking about such things. Of course we are going to die one day. Not today, of course. And not tomorrow. And not even, I should think, next year. I don't," she shifts her hips in her seat, "I don't feel it right now."

Fanny, just starting to come into the room again, makes a noise and leaves, shaking her hands like bird wings over her ears.

"Well, ja, what do you want me to say?" Gerda shouts after her. "I'm not afraid to die! Not me! What is it? It's only nothing. And I can tell you," she turns to us again quickly, "I tell you both, so you can hear—if I die, I want you to take my body and burn it up and throw away the ashes. It will be nothing, my dead body. I don't want to take any more space on this earth. Don't put my dust in the ground, or in an urn, or in a bowl. Just put me over, you know, some roses, or in the sea, or something."

"Okay," Corinne nods. "Whenever you're ready."

"You laugh at me, you—hey, you, funny Corinne! You who can never take things seriously. But this is a serious question I am talking about. Marget thinks we are going to die soon. Shush, *kind!* You know it's true! She says to me, 'I want to tell my children.' But listen. I need to ask you both. Where are your children? Where are your husbands, your houses? I tell you one thing, we are not

going yet, Fan and me, but we are getting old, and a little bit tired. We should like to see a few things before we
leave. We should like to see this much, before we die. Is
it so much to ask?"

"I'm *practicing*, Gerda. But if you want to put more
pressure on . . ." Corinne nudges me with an elbow in
the stomach. It's so sharp, I almost jump away.

"Why can't you ever be serious, hey? Why can't you
wipe that look from your face? It's something, I tell you,
to have children! To have something to live for, to pass
on. You still have time, Marget, maybe, if you are very
lucky, but you, Corinne, no. It's too late for you."

"You don't know that!"

"Bah!"

"But Gerda." Now seems a good time to test the
waters. "Maybe Corinne doesn't want to have children.
Maybe her life isn't going to turn out that way. Maybe
she'll end up differently—like you."

Gerda turns wide eyes toward me.

"Oh? And what makes you think so, *kind?* What
makes you ask that? I know a lot of things, Marget. I
have seen, in my life, a lot of things. And you know what
I think? I think you are speaking for yourself now. You
tell me now, *kind.* You tell me why it is you don't like to
have any children."

I sit facing her, turned inside out, like a goldfish that's
swallowed its bowl. But she's only guessing, poking at
me, snooping around, probing for a spot that will flush
me out. Gerda thinks everyone in the world has a simple answer to give her. She thinks everything's a game

with the cards marked clearly in red and black. She wants me to play.

"I don't know what you mean," I say carefully.

"You see?" Gerda raises her hands and her voice to the ceiling. "Look at what I tell you! Look at that! She doesn't want to have children!"

She brings her head down, as if to drop the sky on me. You are unnatural, her narrowed eyes tell me. You are wasteful, withholding life.

"Why not?" she persists.

"Oh, leave her alone," Corinne interrupts.

"Shush! This is my house. And if I want to know what's going on in it, I can ask. And I want to know why such a pretty young girl doesn't even have a husband yet."

"I'm only twenty-two."

"It's a good age."

"I don't want to quit dancing," I lie.

"No, there's more."

"Just leave her alone, I'm telling you!"

"Shush! You tell me the truth, now!"

No, Gerda. No. I am not going to tell you. I'm not even going to tell you that there is nothing to tell, not yet. The truth is—what? That this is a family of people who fly away from each other like an explosion of chemicals that don't mix. That I'm not even sure, sometimes, how we all manage to fit together. And here I am, just trying to sit and think, calmly, rationally, in the middle of all of you. "I don't know," I say again, more clearly. "I'm just not ready yet. I'm not up for this kind of responsibility."

"Not ready?" Gerda's voice is incredulous. "Bah. In my life I am always ready for anything." And she holds up her wrists, crossed on an imaginary racket, in front of her.

Fan comes in again, soundlessly, and sits down on the curved loveseat beside Gerda. Her body folds almost imperceptibly toward her. It's as if she's trying to be protective.

"We only like to see little babies!" she sings out.

"Oh, just back off Marget now, the both of you!" Corinne gets up nervously, rippling like a loose sail. "You're just being two nosy old *ouwetjes* today."

"Sit!" Gerda points to the spot Corinne has just left. "Sit!" Corinne does, surprisingly. "Now, you listen to me. So maybe Fan likes to see her daughter, and her granddaughter, and maybe her great-granddaughter one day. Is that such a terrible thing? Maybe I like to see you, because you are my brother's child. We *like* you. We like to have you here. We came to America with you, you children, to give you a future, a strong, good beginning."

"No way, Gerda. It wasn't only for us."

"All right, Corinne. Maybe it was also some for me. But only for me so that I could give to you."

I think of the old house, the way Gerda enlarged and encircled and contained it. The way she planted the trees, and sowed the wide lawn, and made a space big enough to meet all her expectations. The way I tore at the three sighing birches.

"And you should know something else, Corinne. Your mother, she died to give you life. Oh, ja. You go on, you roll your eyes, you shake your head. I know you, you don't even like to think about it. You don't even know about that kind of power. Marget, I will tell you instead. When we first came to Holland just after the war, my brother's wife was already sick. She had the tuberculosis, just the same as my Rollie, and the doctor in Holland said to my brother, Listen, you can't let her have any children. You take her away, somewhere warm, to Italy, or to Spain, and you stay there, and you keep yourself off from her. Do you understand? But later that same year, my sister-in-law got herself pregnant. She wanted to have his baby—so badly, you see. And so for all nine months she was in bed spitting up blood, and my brother, he was crying, he was so ashamed of himself.

"So then, when the time came, you can imagine—it went very badly for my sister-in-law. She was screaming for two days. And finally, when the doctor came out, he said to my brother, 'Well, which one do you want to save? The mother, or the child?' And of course my brother said, 'The mother.'"

I look at Corinne. But her breathing hasn't missed a beat. Her face doesn't show a flicker of what it must mean to have someone tell you you were chosen not to be. I erase Corinne from the room. Then I bring her back again. So this is what surviving flesh looks like. This is how we come out, if we come out at all. Flawed, and mysterious, and isolated.

"So they pulled the baby out." Gerda jerks with her hands. "With the forceps—those long ones. And the doctor, he says later it was a miracle. Because Corinne was all right. Perfect. Healthy. Even though when the afterbirth came, it was full—how do you say it?—full of the bacilli of the disease. But Corinne was clean. She took only the good things from her mother.

"Of course they had to take the baby right away. It was too dangerous for her even to be in the room. But my sister-in-law, when she knew she was dying, she begged to see her child. Just once, she wanted to see her, and to touch her. So the doctor agreed. They put the tent over her bed with the oxygen, and they gave her the mask to wear, and gloves. They brought the little baby in, who also had to wear a mask. Then they put the baby's face up against the tent—that was you, Corinne —and my sister-in-law, she was able to feel her baby, just once, for a moment, through the plastic. Then they took Corinne away. And my sister-in-law died."

We sit. Silenced.

"So sad," Fanny whispers, her throat hoarse.

"Yes." Corinne straightens suddenly, dry eyed. She looks grim. "So sad. That someone had to be born that way. That Mama died, and Daddy died, but not me. So sad. That it's only me. So sad. So sad. That I survived."

"Me too," Fanny nods. "Me too."

"So what Gerda is really saying—" Corinne turns to me, but with a greenish smile, and a tinge that looks like copper around her mouth, "—what Gerda is really saying is that in some ways, it was all my fault. That Mama wouldn't have died if she hadn't had me, and Daddy wouldn't have died if Mama hadn't gone first."

"No! That is not what I'm saying."

"So what I'm supposed to do is go out and somehow make up for all that—right, Gerda? I'm supposed to go out and find a man, and make it even. Isn't that the score? Like I've got this great big I.O.U. written up there in the sky somewhere, hanging over me. Or maybe you've got it written down in one of your accounting books, hey Gerda? Maybe you've even tried to pay that one for me, a time or two. It's weird, you know, Marget," she faces me again, "but she thinks she can pay for anything. Even babies. It doesn't really work out that way, does it?"

"It's not your fault!" Fan says hurriedly. "It wasn't my fault!"

"It doesn't matter. Forget it. I'll see you later. I'm out of here." She picks up her purse and jams her bracelets up on her arms, angrily. "You know what I think? We've got fucking too many orphans in this family."

"Corinne!"

It's hard to untangle what happens, quickly, next. Fanny is running, weeping, toward the door, trying to catch and hold and kiss Corinne before she goes. Gerda is coming up behind them, like a wounded bear, trying not to look at anyone, shifting her back on her cane. Corinne holds out a hand, without a word: Gerda reaches into her pocket and hands a roll of folded dollars over to her. I watch the scene as though from the back of an opera house, my eyes straining to make out the pantomime, the words no one is saying.

"Come on, Mag," Corinne calls suddenly, casually, over their heads. "Walk me to my car, why don't you?"

Outside the night is cool, the stars are motionless, clear. Insects are hurtling themselves against the street lights. Corinne starts to put the canvas top up on her convertible, then changes her mind and jerks it back down. She could be ripping off the head of a live animal.

"Okay," she says. "I'm rolling."

She climbs in—flashing a bit of long, pantyhoseless thigh. She reaches out, grabbing my hand in hers, and squeezing it.

"So I'll see you again next time, right?"

"Right. I'm sorry, Corinne."

"What? For all that back in there? Ah, no, don't worry about it, it's nothing. They just drive me a little crazy, sometimes."

"Me too."

Her eyes look hard at me. She seems to doubt it.

"Well . . . okay, but watch out for Fan for me, could you? She's looking so—I don't know. She's got circles under her eyes. She needs to get her heart checked again. Tell Gerda—just tell Gerda to take her to the doctor. Don't say I said so. I just have a feeling. . . . And take care of yourself too, all right? You look a little pale, Mag. Don't let them get you down. You don't have to stay here, I don't care what your mother or anyone else says."

"It's okay. I kind of need to be here, right now."

"Poor you." She turns to fix her smudged mascara in the rearview mirror.

"So you know what all that was about?" She rearranges her face.

"All that in there?"

"Yeah." She stares at me out of her reflection. "All that." She switches her gaze again to redraw her mouth in two sweeping red arcs. But I can still see it, that something blazing, the smoldering anger in the corner of her eyes.

"You remember all those guys I went off and married?"

"Yeah?"

"They were great guys, you remember. Real fun guys. Happening. Bikers. We had such good times. Good times!" She shakes her head. "Even though, maybe, one or two were a little bit crazy. But then, all of a sudden, they'd just go bad on me. Just like that. Want me to quit working, out of nowhere, and wear an apron, and settle down with them, just like *I Love Lucy*. I mean, I just couldn't understand it. What would these guys want to have to do with dirty diapers? And then finally, I figured it out." She points a red fingernail toward the house.

"Oh, come on." It's just too twisted to imagine. "You don't know that."

"No, not for certain." She puts the keys in the ignition. "But I wouldn't put it past her. She's got a lot of money tucked away, that miser. Who's to say she didn't put them up to it? Knock Corinne up, get a bundle from granny. She's got a mind like a criminal, that Gerda. You know, when we first came to America, she had this fake accounting diploma made for herself? Like from Indonesia. It looked so real. And she told everyone she was thirty-five. Thirty-five! And they believed her. She

can lie through her teeth if she has to. She'll do anything. But hey, one day we'll get even with her, right?"
She starts the car.

I nod reassuringly. Corinne winks at me and throws
the car in reverse, flinging her arm over the torn uphol-
stery beside her.

"Well, what do they know about men anyway!" she
shouts. "Couple of crazy old lesbians."

❖ Chapter Nine ❖

My aunt wasn't always so cynical. In her younger days, her laugh didn't have that kind of edge, and she seemed open to almost anything, standing next to my mother with her hair piled up and her neckline pulled down, throwing an arm around Mama as though they were best friends from school, while Mama squinted and hunched and looked as if my tante were a ball and chain slung around her neck. I used to imagine I could see some resemblance between them. I made much of their same dark hair, the fact that they both had pencilled black eyebrows, that they both liked shiny vinyl purses and wouldn't drink wine (Corinne drinks beer), that they were almost the same height and the same weight, and that both were stubborn toward Gerda but careful with Fan.

But the truth is that I couldn't glue my aunt and mother together, because they always kept coming apart. Mama kept reminding me they weren't blood relations, and showed it in the way she looked at Corinne, sideways, like a donkey you posed with at a fair. Corinne kept reminding me by telling me everything about herself my mother wouldn't, and making me her temporary sister when Mama was off and away.

In this way I learned something about Corinne's childhood. And also the story of Oom Bung.

When Corinne was seven years old and the family first came to America, she spent most of her time alone. She tried hanging around with the grown-ups, who were at least old, familiar pillars, but as she ran in and out between their pants and skirts, she only kicked up their tempers, like sand. "Go now," she was told, sometimes harshly, by Gerda or Pip. "Go now and don't bother us anymore, right now. Go find somewhere else to be playing." Because so much had to be done, in the beginning, when they first arrived.

There was the Danish furniture to unwrap and find a place for, and a new set of routines to be established, and garbage to be taken out, and dead thistles to have pulled up from the grassless front yard of the pink house. There were appliances to buy, with their new electric current; and new foods to be bought and stored away and eaten, then bought again and stored away and eaten, and bought again.

After a while Corinne decided it was a good thing to stay out of everyone's way. She tasted her first freedom outside the little pink house, in the vacant lots, in the middle of the streets, running along with the other kids beside the ice cream trucks when they came playing their music-box tunes after school. At dark she would have to come home again, but she came in later and later, simply ignoring Gerda and Fanny and Pip, running in under their scoldings. For her punishment she sometimes had to sit still in a corner while my mother got to go off on a date; Corinne slouched and watched Gerda and Fan and Pip and Elly play their endless card games, practicing their terrible, stuttering English.

But on some nights, when the house was quiet and the sky hung low without a moon, Gerda would clear the cards away and call them all to a seance. "Go to sleep," Corinne was told then. "Go now, it's time for you to be in your room." So Corinne's first definition of seance was: something we don't want you to see.

Elly and Pip would turn off the lights. Fanny would light a single white candle. And Corinne, because she no longer did what she was told, would slip quietly out of her bed to hide behind the loveseat and watch them.

A special seance was always held on the eighth day of May. That was Oom Bung's birthday. Corinne had had to ask, once, who exactly Oom Bung was. Crazy Tante Elly, with her sleepy eyes wandering, had kindly sat Corinne down and told her. "Oom Bung is our half-Chinese great uncle," Elly said. "He died in a typhoon on Java one night, when his roof collapsed and fell like a stone on top of him. To die that way leaves you irritable and unhappy—you still have so many things you want to talk about. A sudden death makes you easy to reach. With Oom Bung, death jumped out at him, like a tiger." But—did Oom Bung die on his birthday? Corinne asked. "No," Tante Elly said. "But it's good to call them that day. Even dead people like attention on their birthdays."

And so, on the eighth day of May, in the tiny pink house lit with one candle, the four women sat around the table and joined hands. Fanny's words went up with an echoing sound like bells, and Corinne imagined that her not-mother had somehow swallowed a voice that was not her own.

"Oom Bung, we call you now to come back to us."

"Oom Bung, we want to feel you in space."

"Oom Bung, blow the candle if you can be near us."

And Gerda and Pip and Elly replied:

"Oom Bung!"

"Oom Bung!"

"Oom Bung!"

Corinne sneezed loudly behind the loveseat. The four women jumped up and stood looking around them, cursing until they found her and pulled her out. Now they would have to begin all over again.

"And I was just beginning to feel him."

"You too? What did he feel like?"

"Like something heavy inside my head."

"Like stones."

"Go to bed now," Fanny said in her old voice.

They pushed Corinne back down the hallway and into her room.

But Corinne didn't sleep. She sat up in bed, twisting the sheet like a snake between her legs. Fanny's deep ringing calls came again, and again, heavy, invisible, falling in waves against the door.

"Oom Bung, can you see us?"

"Oom Bung, show your face."

"Oom Bung."

"Oom Bung."

"Oom Bung."

Corinne crept into the hallway. Their four heads were thrown back. Their hands shook. They looked like four devils chained together.

Gerda noticed her.

"What is it *now*?"

"I have to go to the w.c. You didn't let me go the w.c., first."

She had gone, of course, already, before. But the only thing she wanted now was to break the chain. To stop their strange, sullen voices, the breathing, and all the moaning, all the clutching, like shipwrecked sailors, in the middle of the night.

"Go on. We will wait for you."

She went and took as long as she could, holding back her stream. But finally she had to come out.

"Good. Now go to sleep."

There was silence then, for a long time. Then the calls came softly again, getting up, loping, like an animal through the house. Then more silence, more silence, more silence. Or was it? She was beginning to hear something pumping, a pounding inside her ears.

Gerda and Fan must be waiting for something. But what? A spirit? A demon? A ghost? Would the candle blow out, would the table come off the floor, wobbling, like everyone said Fan could still do? Although of course Corinne had never once seen it. The silence grew gigantic, like a bubble. She couldn't stand it. She couldn't breathe. She had to break it. She shrieked.

Her door was being flung open, and now something monstrous stood in the dark in front of her, a huge, panting, shapeless beast with four heads, all nodding and bobbing, breathing, all staring at her with wide open, yellow-looking eyes. Its four mouths hung open like Venus flytraps.

"Tell us!" it said. "Tell us what you saw!"

She tried feeding it. "A man."

"A man? What sort of man? What did he look like?"

"Old. Chinese. With a—cake."

"What did he look like? Was he tall or short? Was he short, would you say?"

"He was sitting, down there. Like a rabbit." She could almost see him.

"Did you notice what he was wearing?"

"Black."

"Can you say what he was doing?"

"He was looking at me. He—smiled?"

"Then he was gone?"

"Then he was gone."

They all exhaled.

Now the monster came apart. Her mothers and aunts all laughed. "Look how scared she is!" Gerda and Pip and Elly said, and poked one another. "That old Bung. He always liked to scare children, remember? He was always playing his tricks." The three of them went back down the hallway.

"Come, *poppeke,*" Fan said, tucking Corinne gently into bed. "You should try to go to sleep now."

Corinne learned, that night, that people will often give you a sign when there is something they badly want from you. That it's easy to follow that sign, and give them what they want, and keep yourself for yourself, safely hidden. When for years afterward they kept telling her she was a wild and terrible girl who wouldn't listen, Corinne, I'll bet, liked being a wild and terrible girl who wouldn't listen, in this way making everyone happy. But with my mother, it was like writing a book and finding out the title had two meanings. She always did everything my grandmothers told her she should. She was good, she worked hard, she did her lessons, she got married, she had a baby, she grew up, she left them. And only later, they found out, that's not what they had meant at all.

Chapter Ten

My first memories of my mother are of a face as soft and pink and cool as a melon and hair so deeply black above me that in the sunlight it went peacock with blue. She wore it long when she was young, below her shoulders, curled under, but when I was five years old she cut it all off, so short it looked like the buzzes the soldiers on television wore. My grandmothers both wailed when they saw her new 'do. To this day they hate it. They say it makes her look like a prisoner in a concentration camp.

I couldn't see at first that for this and many other reasons my mother wasn't beautiful. To me she was an angel, a snowbird like in the song, a high, vaulted light I could only look up to. When the years began taking beauty away from my mother's face, it had nothing to do with the lines that were scratching themselves like hieroglyphs around her mouth. It was only life itself, pulling back its veils. Revealing to me that the thing in the world I loved first was not the first thing in the world.

My mother was like my grandmother. Like Fanny, she cared for the house. Like Fanny's, her body was light and fine-boned, though Mama's muscles were firmer and rounder, harder underneath her short clothing; and her skin, because she didn't use powder, showed more of the Javanese color running underneath it, embedded in a stronger, deeper sediment. When she came home at night from the bakery, throwing off her sticky work dress, she would hurry and cook for us a fat, steaky, American dinner, then clean up right behind us, sopping things up, erasing our tracks. Then she sat down and began her embroidery.

Mama's hobby was cross-stitching. She sewed parrots with long, scything tails, flowers in perfect bunches, stallions and butterflies and Spanish dancers. She bought the patterns at Woolworth's. But they were only a framework to start with. The first time around, she followed the instructions exactly, staying carefully inside the lines, using all the right-colored threads. She obeyed the printed borders on the meshing like a map, her stitches columning up and down, racing, like mathematical figures. She finished one elegant Spanish dancer this way: the red flounces just right, the almond skin even-toned, the body curved like a gourd. Mama framed her finished dancer, and then hung it on the living room wall. We all sat looking up at it, while she started over again.

But she didn't copy it properly. She didn't keep count of the stitches. She started changing the shapes, the colors, using bloody browns for the reds, oranges for the almonds, violent purples, blues and magentas, blacks, the parrot's leftover yellows and greens. The round, kissing mouth of the dancer became jagged, uneven, her raised arms grew stiff like dead tree branches, her body blockish, like a pile of empty cartons. Mama would make another and another copy this way, each one growing more confusing, more altered than the last. But *Mama*, I complained, why can't you do it the *same way* every time? Why can't you make them all match? Make things look right again!

But Mama said only: That's boring. She framed each of her four Spanish dancers, and hung them all over the house. It was like looking at Mr. Hyde, in stages. When they grew faded and dusty she put them all away, lining the bottoms of drawers with them, or storing them in the garage. Mama doesn't let many things linger.

Her books were different. They came over with her on the boat from Holland when she was still young. She had my father build modular shelves for them in the living room, where she divided them by subject, keeping them in exactly the same order, in beds like oysters, some of them already crusted and yellow-brown. The oldest were from her days as a student in Holland. She loved European history then, and Hollywood, and Greece and Rome. Her *Ivanhoe* still had pasted magazine photos of Liz and Robert Taylor inside it; her medieval and Roman histories were brailled from where she'd carefully colored in the black-and-white sketches of wimples and battlements. The histories were written in Dutch, so I was never able to read them—I peeked into the Greek picture books instead. I wondered at the men's drooping testicles, so strange and ungodlike. At the snake-haired gorgon woman, her face broken open, splaying, like a hungry anemone. I flinched when I saw the Medusa: Mama had told me all about her. One unprotected look and the monster would turn you into stone.

Mama had saved her ballet books from her lessons at the Dutch conservatory. They were full of black-and-white photos, crisp and clear. Russian girls posed with huge white bows spread like pinwheels on the sides of their heads. Tall women balanced on their toes, pointing toward the sky, captured like frozen fountains inside their slippers. In some pictures the ballerina was held up by a strong, broad arm, and you could see the wide hand around her waist, thick and supporting her, so firm, so tender, so trustworthy.

Mama was surprised when I begged for ballet lessons. She wasn't sure about it, at first. She told me how Fanny had had lessons too, when she was young. That made me part of a perfect line. It was like being handed the key to an already built kingdom, a Camelot, an Athens, a Rome. It would be like crawling inside the warmest, softest, most perfectly pink sea-god's shell.

There is comfort in being one of a company. Standing backstage, each thin figure hums with electric preparation. The muscles strain, the chins tilt upward. There is a tension, a rhythmic yearning and envy between adrenalin-filled bodies. In a moment they will take the stage, sustaining by sheer force of will the shape of something light, an effervescence. A touch. A pose. We melt and are gone. This much I learned, quickly: a dancer can never make herself permanent.

Standing in the resin box before my entrance. What is it I once loved about dancing? Not the motion. Not the music. It was the stillness before. The shared purpose, the concentration, the joined preparations. The looks of encouragement, nervousness, pain, anxiety, whispered words of luck, fingers crossed, voodoo signs. Some dancers trace the shape of a cross with the tip of each toe on the stage floor before their entrance. Others, every night, do the same number of grandes battements, right and left. The corps de ballet exchange swear words, and laugh. The men jump up and down in one place, straining to their hairlines, pulling themselves up by their roots, higher and higher.

I stand in the resin box, the lights soaring above me like dragons. I coat my pink slippers with dust, grinding in my heels until they are thick, resistant, hard, and sticky. To fall would be the worst nightmare. No: to forget, to lose your place in the music. To get lost in the conductor's dream. Every night, the same old terrors.

I am trained. I am terrified. I stand at the very edge of the wings. The wings are the edge of a world. Behind them is safety, half-darkness, invisibility. Beyond them is a hot, hallowed place, electric. You can feel the boundary, like a wall in front of you, invisible, permeable, but real.

The orchestra tunes itself. The sound raises the hair on my arms.

"House lights to half, please."

"One minute, dancers."

"Places, please, dancers. Quiet, please."

The corps lines the wings.

"House lights out."

Applause for the conductor. A careful ear, a frightened one, can pick out the soft tapping of the violins. Now everything is silent. The stage manager whispers into his headset. The still, curtained stage begins to glow.

"Merde," a corps girl whispers beside me.

"Merde," I whisper back.

Music. The curtain rises. Chins up. A part of me can still hear the stagehands hauling on the ropes.

The next thing is to go out and find it. I have to go out, and find the glowing red light.

I picked him out during rehearsals from the tangle of competing bodies. Taller than the rest, regal, a prince— but loose and sleek as a fish. The muscles in his back and legs were matching, cupped, as though left by the halves of a broken mold. This was the first time I can remember feeling dizzy with desire, overwhelmed by standing close to something so perfect.

I plotted to have this beautiful, perfect thing. I threw myself in front of him as though he were a speeding train. We brushed shoulders as we bent down to pick up our dance shoes. A few weeks later we were going home together.

We were competitive. We pushed ourselves forward to the front of every class; side by side, we took the most prominent positions at the barre. I watched him out of the corner of my eye. He was so blond and promising, with beautiful feet, arched like a woman's, sensual and hairless. I was surprised by our lovemaking at first. It was all very spontaneous and unchoreographed and disappointing. I wanted it to be like dancing: an effortless pas de deux. But he only laughed and pinched my thigh when I told him. Come on, he said, let's go take a bath.

In a studio of fifty dancers the air becomes murky with sweat. Bodies glisten. Curves become clear. I was always staring, at everyone. I saw two men on the floor, wrestling, laughing, joyous, two lovers playing, flaunting their indulgence in each other's bodies. I never saw female dancers playing that way. But then I knew why. There are far too many of us. For too few roles. Our brief touches were charged, opposing.

In the mirror we adjusted our rehearsal skirts and measured each other's bodies. Many were more perfect than mine. The ideal female dancer is womanly for her unwomanliness, small-breasted, thin, hipless, and strong. With the illusion of weakness. And white. I was never, to any of the costumers' minds, white enough. For the great snowy ballets, *Swan Lake* and *Giselle*, I was told to blend in, powder down. In the dressing room I coated my skin with a layer of pale pancake, then finished it off with talcum, closing myself like a seal. In the mirror I saw a stranger: a ghostly zombie girl.

My lover wasn't unfaithful, precisely. He didn't teach me anything about staying in love. He did show me something about lust, about falling so far down into something delirious, delicious, you can only look up afterward at your life as it was before, like a navel drawn up tight against the sky.

One of the first things you learn as a dancer is how to "spot." To spot is to fool your body. It's to keep your head fixed in one position while the rest of your body turns, then snap it, flashing around, to catch up with yourself again. This is how a dancer keeps from getting dizzy. One turn equals one spot. Two turns—two spots.

My first ballet teacher was a small woman with wiry, silvery hair curled in tight buttons beside her ears. Edwina had once danced in Paris. She kept her studio filled with pictures of herself, as La Sylphide, as Sleeping Beauty, as Juliet, tacking herself all over the walls of her converted two-car garage. She breezed in on Saturday mornings like a gypsy, wearing a long black spangled shawl for a skirt. Come, she said briskly, pushing us in a group toward the mirrors. Today we are going to learn our pirouettes. And she settled our small round shoulders just as if she were arranging onions on a cart.

Now, she said. You must always look *forward*. You must always pay *attention*. You must try not to lose sight of your *face*. Like this! Look in the mirror. Spot and turn! See yourself again. Again. Spot and turn! See yourself. Spot and turn! Spot and turn!

We wound our bodies carefully, twisting them like springs. We learned to snap back, like rubber bands, locking on the targets of our eyes. Edwina nodded, approvingly. Then she turned us all away from the mirrors. We were spotting next on the knots in the wooden paneling of the garage. We spotted on Edwina herself, on her nose, on her raised finger, on the skin hanging from under her arm, as translucent and veined as a butterfly's wing.

But now, she said. You say to yourself: What will I do when I get on the stage? What will I do when there is no more mirror, no more finger, no more wall for my face to look into? I won't lie to you—it's frightening. It's a terrible thing. You will feel like you have no balance. You will feel like you're going to fall, down, down, down, right into the orchestra pit. But you have two choices before this happens. You can look inside yourself. Do you see what I mean? You can imagine, inside your head, the face you always saw in the mirror. You can spot from inside your head. Does that sound too difficult? Then you can do this. You can look for the little red shining light. They will hang it for you, the ballerina, a red light at the very center and back of the house, under the balcony. Find this, and you will have your spot again. That's enough. Now let's practice our jetés.

When I come on, always, I have to look first for the red light. From the stage it looks just like a drop of warm blood, hanging steady, suspended, never falling. It's the light of the coast that's going to keep you from drowning. It's the heat to melt the fear in your bones.

We spent hours, my lover and I, glazed, tired, groaning and sweating, alone up in his big, empty loft. We wrestled in the middle of his sagging double bed, lying afterwards, sore, under the breeze from his open window. Isn't it amazing, we said, how well we go together? I can't imagine anything as perfect as this, anything so absorbing as this. Can you? I can't imagine anything being so intense.

We talked a great deal about how meaningful our talks were.

I think we rubbed up so much against each other we finally wore the gilt off. I started to come out of the deep place gradually, like a diver returning sensibly to air. When we went our separate ways, a few months later, it was all right, no bad feelings, we were friends. My last image of my lover is the back of his head, inside a taxi, growing smaller down my street, disappearing in the direction of the airport.

I went back to rehearsals, to classes. I thought I'd returned to normal. When I found out, a few weeks later, it was like being sucked backward into a whirlpool. I couldn't remember it, retrace it, the channel, the path—the way we had both come so cleanly out. We had done everything we were supposed to do. We'd taken all the usual safeties and precautions, worn all the right jackets and preservers. And then suddenly, there it was, puckering in surprise at me: a small round *o* at the bottom of the tube. The gravity was fierce looking down. I could already feel it, real, powerful, already a foregone conclusion, pulling me in through its center.

I decided I would say nothing. To anyone. This thing was mine now, to have and to hold. To hold up to the light like a prism, a problem, and see all its flashes of hot and cold and neutral colors. I needed to get out, get away, to have some place to think—but where? How?

I tried to make myself serene. More perfect, more lightfooted, more silent across the stage, more insubstantial than a dead leaf falling, so light and thin that if you turned me to one side you could see right around me, like a weathervane. This, I realize now, was all that I'd managed to learn.

At the end of the final performance of a season, dancers like to linger on the stage. Old jealousies are forgotten behind the sudden drop of the curtain, behind the red velvet guillotine that means the end of an era, an hour, a place. I remember our voices rising like feathers, loosening out of our costumes, floating up into the rafters. Where are you going? What are you doing? Have you signed a new contract? Will you be coming back?

No. I'm going home to California. I think the air out there will do me good.

Outside the theater was all coldness and dark. The audience, glittering, forgetful, hungry, had evaporated into taxis and waiting limousines. I just stood there, my heavy bag loaded with worn-out shoes, and wondered at all the stillness, all the silence. It's difficult at the end of any season to know how to feel.

Chapter Eleven

My grandmother is growing anxious. Tiny things give her away, like the way she's pouring Gerda's still-warm coffee down the food disposal. Yesterday she threw a pair of Gerda's dark blue socks in with the white wash, staining all of our underwear a faint, marine green.

I've tried to talk to her about the operation, explain how simple it is, but she only tenses and then slips away from us like a mole into the holes of her eyes. At least she's no longer worried about Corinne. My grandmothers forget everything as soon as the exhaust fades from their cul-de-sac. They will probably forget me, too, when I leave. They'll be sitting once again alone beside each other, like one-eyed cards, king and queen, facing each other, but looking away.

My grandmother sits at the end of her kitchen table, her milky coffee spinning like a cloudy oracle in front of her. She stares over her wrist into that place that is not herself.

I wonder, sometimes, if this is how she'll finally leave us. Simply sink down into the table, melting like ice, or collapse, with a soft sound, like dried leaves inside her clothing. Will we sweep her into a dustpan, the way Mama does? I can imagine Gerda's face, stoic, hardened, accepting. I try to imagine what Mama will do, how she will finally have to come home again. Yes, she will have to come home.

I know my parents have hoped, for a long time now, that of the two of them Fan will be the first to go. How would she even survive, they wonder, without Gerda to clothe and shelter her? Who will be there to shield her from the outside world? If Fanny dies first, they reasonably say, Gerda will still find her way. She might get lost in the kitchen, she might have to live on TV dinners, but nothing worse, nothing a microwave couldn't fix. She lived alone, once before, while Fanny was in the hospital with angina, and made her meals off bananas and canned sodas. When a Boy Scout came to the door selling wooden-spoon sets, she simply told him to come back another day. When the lady of the house would be at home.

Gerda would coil her thick fingers around whatever problem faced her, and force it down and underneath her, making it a foothold. She would probably even like a little adversity, coming this late in her old life. Gerda confronts Minute Rice, Gerda faces down Quaker Quick Oats. New opponents to be conquered, beaten, and eaten.

But for Fanny—for poor Fanny, the loneliness would be terrible. There would be darkness even in daylight, and strange, unseen webs gilding the world. No, Gerda shook her head at me once, your grandmother is going to be in trouble. Right now she can hardly even leave the house. When I have to take her out to the bank, once a month, to deposit her Social Security, she is shaking all night, sick with worry, and she can hardly get dressed in the morning. How can a person like this, I ask you, Marget, live alone in this world?

Yet I know Gerda is preparing for just that. She's arranged to have all her assets put in trust, to be dribbled out to Fan, in transfusions, each month. Of course, Gerda said, her inheritance taxes will be terrible because, even after forty years, the government still says we are not a family.

Corinne will inherit everything after my grandmother has died: the money, the car, the milk-company shares, the house. All this, Gerda shrugged, she will lose in six months.

My grandmother sits and broods over her coffee, as if none of this could enter her traveled mind. A cough, low in her chest, shakes her like a bough. She notices me.

"How are you feeling, Oma? Maybe you should go lie down?"

"*Nee*, it's all right. *Bedankt*, Marget."

"There's nothing to worry about." I take her by the

hand. "I keep telling you. It's not a difficult thing. Gerda isn't nervous."

Under each of her tender eyes is a black, berryish swelling.

"Gerda is nervous."

I can't tell it when Gerda finds me, sitting at the roll-away bar. The vinyl stool sighs softly underneath her. The tiny liquor bottles, leftovers from my mother's long flights, jingle like potions on an alchemist's desk.

"What are you doing, *kind?*"

I set the letter I'm holding smoothly aside. "I thought you wouldn't mind if I sat here."

"No, it's okay, we don't use this now. We are so old, we can't drink. Who are you writing to, then?

"Not writing. Just reading."

"Ah. I never write letters, me. Too much work. I think it's better to say something to a person's face. A letter is too much like a question."

She stares down at the paper I've hidden.

"Ja!" she says suddenly, as if remembering something. "You should be coming outside now, Marget! We are going to sit in the yard, on a nice day like this. The roses are popping, like fireworks. You should come and sit with us, in the sun, and stop all this writing."

"I will in just one minute."

"You should come with us now."

"I'll be out in just a bit, I promise."

"Ja. But listen, *kind.*"

She stares down at the nub of her cane, picking it with her thumbnail.

"Don't write anything about my operation."

"Of course not."

"Good." She straightens. "So. I'll see you in the yard in one minute."

"Okay."

I take up the letter again, forwarded with my other mail. It's from my grandfather, written on blue onion-skin airletter, filled with gossipy news, in his lean, pointed Dutch hand. He has a new green parrot they've called Dung For Days. They have had a party for all their Dutch and Afrikaner friends. His dear, pretty wife has had the toothache, and a slight pain in the back of her neck. Their garden is blooming; their maid has been coming late due to trouble on the township trains. The girl was so upset, she forgot to take the reds out when she washed all the whites. His best winter trousers had been ruined, but well, there, then. You know a *kaffer* is getting old when her hair goes gray.

"Your grandfather would like you to write to him." My mother said this to me when I was eight or nine years old, and handed me a piece of blue paper with an airmail stamp on it. Of course I knew I had a grand-father—in theory, like a star. He lived in South Africa. Those two words were all that described him: he was an old white man who moved with a cocked gun be-tween elephants and tigers across green velds. My mother never wrote to him or told him what we were doing; she hasn't seen him in over thirty years and doesn't appear to have happy memories. She still hates the thought of circuses, for instance, and can't even hear them mentioned without shivering and muttering something about horrible people and greasepaint and bear piss.

She told me my grandfather abandoned them after the war. They knew he'd been hauled off with the others into Burma; it was only later they were told he'd probably been shot. But four years after the war he had shown up, out of nowhere, in Rotterdam, alive, perfectly healthy, and carrying a suitcase stamped with all the great cities of Europe. He wore a new suit, and stood on the doorstep of Gerda's three-story Dutch house, asking for Fan and for a divorce and for my mother, all in one ghostly breath.

Fanny had fainted. Gerda had cursed. She drove my grandfather from her house, flinging his legal papers into the street after him. My mother still remembers the arguments that followed, the lawyers, the judges, the tears, the decision, the shrieks shrilling like shattered glass through the house. A year later, my grandmothers finally had to give my eleven-year-old mother up, and Han came and took her away, to spend the summer traveling with him, a perfect stranger.

I don't think my mother has ever forgiven Gerda or Fan. She had to spend every school vacation with Han, touring all over the continent watching his clown act. Until one year he finally found his way down to South Africa, with some other Dutch clowns, and settled there, and didn't send for her anymore. She won't talk about her years with the circus now. But all that wandering stuck like fat to her bones.

I don't know why my mother had me write to my grandfather. I don't know why she wanted that faraway, dim, outer link for me, unless it was out of some kind of guilt or fear, maybe the fear of the stranger. The letters my grandfather sends this way from that far, upside-down part of the world aren't especially interesting, or unusual. Except in their hatred. He writes casually of black "bastards" who should be put, as he says, into cages. He seems so assured of his superiority. He seems so to love his new country, his South Africa. He wants to show it to me, he writes, before "they" get everything all mucked up.

My grandmothers sit out on the patio, in the shade of their fold-out umbrella. In their wrought-iron garden chairs they look isolated, peaceful, as distinct from each other as two temples. I wonder sometimes about married life. I wonder what gets telegraphed between those two poles, if what they see is really the same behind those two pairs of eyes—I notice it, sometimes, in my parents. You can tell when two people are pulling the same load. They lean forward, the angles match. Even in sleep.

"Sit down," Gerda smiles. "Sit down, *kind.*" I pull a chair into the shade with them.

We sit for a while, nothing happening, staring down our noses.

"So are you all ready, then, Gerda? All set for your big day tomorrow?"

"Always."

"And are you nervous?"

"*Nee!* Not at all. I have a good man, my doctor. It will all go very smoothly, like sailing." She lifts her chin, as if into a breeze.

"You had a bad dream," Fanny whispers.

"What? What are you saying? Oh. Ja. That is true. But it was only a little nightmare. Only nothing."

We sit quietly for another moment, listening to the distant throttle of a neighbor's lawnmower.

"Well, what was the dream about, Gerda?"

She clinks her heavy signet ring on the arm of the chair. "Well . . . It was strange, really. A kind of ghost-nightmare. I dreamed someone was in our bedroom, last night. A young woman, in the dark, looking down at us. Over our bed. It was a spirit, I think—no, ja—a *kuntianak*. They will come to you, you know, the *kuntianak*, these girls, the ones that die young, like Corinne's mother. They come to you when they are wanting something, something to do for their children. But I wasn't sure exactly what it was. So I felt for Fan, and I shook her and I said, 'Wake up! Wake up! Look, here is someone beside our bed! Looking at you!' But Fan said only, 'You're crazy, go back to sleep.' She didn't even look to see the woman. But I can almost see her. Small. Lost. And hungry. But then, when I blink to see her better, she is gone.

"Well," Gerda says, sounding her ring again on her chair like a bell. "I think we should go inside now."

Fan helps her up from the chair, brushing off the iron-grill pattern on Gerda's back. As soon as she's able, Gerda shakes her off, planting her stick with a thunk like a club in the yard.

"Bah!" She digs in. "When I come home on Friday, there will be no more of this! No more walking around on three legs! I will have my new knee, my strong one, made of steel. Then you will see, Fan, how strong I will be. Then you will watch me dance around here."

"Yes, Vent," my grandmother says quietly, sliding the patio door closed softly behind us.

❧ Chapter Twelve ❧

On the way to the hospital Gerda sits in the passenger seat beside me and wraps her wide thumbs around her purse. She's asked me to drive, feeling the importance of what's about to happen to her, setting herself apart like a virgin poised at the edge of a volcano. She stares out the window at the passing shopping malls, at the people waiting for buses underneath Plexiglas shelters. From the corner of my eye I watch her watching. She turns her head slightly, blinking at them. Her face looks blank, almost lineless in the morning light. Only the pink, frowning crease of her mouth is unchanged. But then this is what I have always suspected about Gerda. It's not for her, this mystical communion with souls unknown. For Gerda, other people are complete mysteries.

"Slow down now, *kind*. It's next on the right."

Her huge station wagon responds stiffly, like a freight car stuck on its rails. As we turn I catch a glimpse of Fanny in the rearview mirror, looking small and unhappy. She doesn't like driving. It makes her motion-sick. Her lips are pursed around a piece of sugared licorice, the fragile muscles of her face quietly clenching.

By coincidence we saw a procedure nearly exactly like Gerda's performed last night on a medical documentary. The patient, a sleeping, white-haired woman of about sixty-five, lay dormant, like a hill, the plastic oxygen tube standing like a heavy reed in her mouth. The lower half of her body lay hidden behind a curtain of green. On the other side a second camera picked up the already prepared knee: it lay exposed like an orchid between layers of gauze and plastic. With one unflourished cut the surgeon had sliced under this woman's skin, springing the jaundiced cap off like the cover of an antique pocketwatch.

The flesh underneath was purple and bloodless, the cartilage a brilliant white. The surgeon had handled the flap of the kneecap with a smooth, businesslike affection. He mauled it pleasantly between finger and thumb, showing its size to the camera. He rolled it like a dollar bill, and then flattened it out again. We watched as he rebuilt the joint in steps, using a drill and pins and screws, then testing the mobility of his unconscious patient, working her like a lever, a problem to be solved, bending and straightening, bending and straightening. His matter-of-factness made me queasy.

The nurses bent and applied suction to the wound as it filled with a watery gray liquid. After an hour the doctor finally closed the incision with heavy stitches, tugging at the wet skin until it puckered.

Fanny left the room with a napkin pressed to her mouth. Gerda sat back and said it really looked quite simple.

It's Gerda, hobbling, frowning, who leads us through the hospital lobby past the colorful hot-air balloons pictured on the walls. The nurse clears the appointment and hands Gerda insurance and release forms. Gerda gives her cane wordlessly to Fan, and sits backward into the wheelchair the orderly has rolled under her. She grips its plastic armrests; it looks if she's trying to hold a set of jaws apart. She looks up at the orderly, registering him.

"Okay," she says uncomfortably. "Let's go."

In the semi-private room we are left alone. The crumpled sheets on one bed give it a deserted, lonesome look. Gerda stares blankly at the bed that isn't hers, then turns, reaching out to touch her own clean, tucked sheets. "Ja," she says. "This one is for me." She slides one hand flat over the bed and then climbs on top of it, gingerly.

I leave her suitcase on the table while Fan looks down the drop outside the window. The palm and eucalyptus trees look gray, smoldering from up here.

"It's so high," Fanny frets.

"Sit down, Fan. *Toch*. You are making me nervous."

My grandmother doesn't move but tries leaning her hip slightly against the window sill.

"So here we go!" I say. It sounds stupid, bright, overdone. I can't help it. There is something about hospital air that makes me dizzy, lightheaded, like on an air-plane. A feeling of breathing in other people's breath-ing, of air that's too fresh to be fresh, too clean to be clean. Somewhere close by, I know, there are newborn babies lying in little Plexiglas cubby beds, little experi-ments gurgling inside their petri dishes. I can't think about it right now. "Just think," I say to Gerda. "Pretty soon it'll all be over. Pretty soon you'll be able to eat whatever you want again."

"I'm so hungry now, I could eat a cat."

"Do you like something?" Fan hovers anxiously. "Do you like something to drink?"

"No. I can only have the water, anyway. Let's just sit here for a minute. Then you have to go."

"*Nee!*" my grandmother wails.

Gerda frowns, shaking her head at me. This, she glares across at Fan, should have been settled a long time ago.

But now she changes tactics. "But see, Fan, see here," Gerda croons, low and sweetly. Her voice sounds like a hot metal rod that's been dipped in icy water. "Marget and I already talked about this. We already decided it. It's going to be too long for you waiting here—all of these preparations, and so on. Too much time for the surgery. You should go home. You should go home, and then the nurse will call you, when I am finished."

"*Nee!*" She sounds almost firm.

"But, Oma, listen," I coax. "I think it's a good idea. The house is so close by. And I'll bring you right over, right afterwards, I promise."

"I want to stay here."

"But you can't!" Gerda pounds the bed now, losing her patience. "What do you want? What are you talking about? You think they are going to let you watch? You think they are going to let you in that room with me? What are you going to do here? Look at you, you don't even like to sit down, you are so scared of the hospital you are afraid to touch it! Are you going to stand up here for three hours? I don't think so. No, Marget, *nee*, you take her home. And Fan, you go and make Marget a good, good lunch."

"*Nee*, Vent. I can't."

"Of course you can. You will like to eat something, when you are at home again."

Gerda holds her purse out for Fan to set on the night-stand, giving her something to do. When Fan's back is turned Gerda mutters to me in Dutch, something about the stubbornness of all weak women. She curls her hands impatiently on her knees, her nails turned under. She's getting anxious. She stares up at the television mounted near the ceiling, as if at a darkened crystal ball. Gerda doesn't like to wait for a thing. She likes to come up to the net, to meet it.

"I'm not nervous," she says again. "I'm strong."

"You are nervous."

"*Nee*. I'm not. I'll be only sleeping. I'm strong, I come from a strong family. My father was strong, my mother was strong. She had eight children, Marget, did you know that? Five boys and three girls. All of my brothers are dead now, but I had to be strong, when they were alive, to get what I wanted in our house."

"Gerda, maybe you should start—"

"Listen to this! Once, when I was little, I wanted to play a game with my brothers. It was something with a ball, something new I learned in school. But they didn't want to play it. They made up a test. They said to me, 'Okay, Gerdie, tell you what. We'll go play your game, if you'll go into the garden and eat one of *kokkie*'s lombok.' Do you know what a lombok is, Marget? It's a pepper. Very hot. Our *kokkie* grew them, for cooking, for making sambals. So I said to my brothers, 'Of course I will, I'll show you chickens, I'm not scared.' And I went into the garden, just like I wasn't afraid. But I was, Marget. Oh, I was afraid. The lombok is like fire. I tried to pull my stomach in tight, like a fist. I tried to open my eyes, like chimneys. Then I took one off, straight off the bush, and I shut my eyes, and I heard a noise that sounded like biting my own finger. Oh, it was terrible, the pain. Oh, so hot. I thought I was going to die. The tears were all coming, burning me. But I didn't cry. I didn't let fall for them one drop. Because I am strong. 'There!' I spit it out. 'Now you have to take one!' But of course my five brothers wouldn't do it. They all ran away. After that, you can imagine, I could play anything I wanted. No one says '*nee*' to me. My parents right away let me have tennis lessons. They died, you know, Marget, before the war. They were lucky. They didn't have to see it."

She seems to be getting worked up. "Maybe you should get changed now, Gerda," I say. "The doctor might be coming soon."

"Ja, you are right." She looks around the room again, noticing, squinting. "Okay. You go on. Someone should be coming to take my blood pressure."

"Vent!" my grandmother pleads again, but seems, on second thought, to know it's useless. She's already bending and kissing Gerda on the cheek.

"Okay, you go with Marget."

I kiss Gerda in turn.

"We'll see you in a little while. Don't make trouble now."

"Very funny. I will have the nurses call you."

She waves us away, and we go. I have to guide Fanny like a mannequin out of the room. We turn back again in the hallway outside the door, but Gerda has already settled her back to us, and sits silhouetted on her bed like a small mountain against the window. She looks calm. My old grandmother. Ready to fight another war. The last war of the old against peace.

At the house everything seems oddly contracted. The furniture looks shrunken, sapped, drawn into itself—the narrow arms of the Danish furniture, the dangling chains of the hanging lamps. The walls have quietly expanded, I notice, like bookends that have been shoved apart. I can feel the difference, and understand it. There is more room in these rooms, without Gerda.

Fanny peeks cautiously into the cavern, but can't bear the empty living room and retreats toward the kitchen. I can hear her, what sounds like her bony hips knocking aimlessly, dejected, against the countertop. But when I come in I find nothing more than the table set neatly for two, and last night's pork and rice already steaming in pots on the stove.

Fan comes out of the pantry with a jar of fresh sambal in her hands, and sets it mechanically between our plates. Her face is wilted. Some of the powder has rubbed off. In the car on the way home she'd sat forlorn beside me, dark, leathery-looking, a turtle without her shell.

Now the problem of the sambal faces me again. I can't eat it. The color alone is enough to make my eyes water: brilliant orange-red, blistering, with oily seeds floating inside, encased in tiny bubbles against the glass. Fan looks at me. She looks at the jar. She looks at me. To please her, I spoon some out and place it safely at the edge of my plate. When she isn't looking I'll scoop it into my napkin and take it and hide it in a wastebasket upstairs.

My grandmother ladles spoon after spoon of the hot sambal over her rice, until her plate is as fiery as a bursting tongue. I've stopped wondering how this is even possible. But Gerda says nothing has enough spice for Fan if she doesn't use the hot sambal.

"Oma," I say suddenly. "Did you used to cook like this, when you were in Surabaya?"

"Oh!" She seems astonished I'm still here. "If I have something to cook. But we had nothing to eat, at the end of the war."

"Because of the Japanese."

"No, no. It wasn't the Japanese. It was the Indonesians. Gerda always found food, with the Japanese."

We continue eating in silence, pushing our spoons and forks together Indies-style.

"How come you never like to talk about it?"

Her eyes are sleepy. But now it seems as if she's really tired.

"Gerda will like to tell you," she smiles mechanically. "Eat more, eat more now, Marget."

While we're washing the dishes, my grandmother doesn't look at me. She's uncomfortable accepting my help, taking even one dirty glass from my hands. She slides the plates I hand her with a nervous flip into the soapy water. She never uses the built-in dishwasher at her knees.

"What about," I try again, "how all of you left Gerda's house? Remember that story? Gerda told me once. But how did you know to go, right then? How did you know it was safe?"

"You can ask Gerda, Marget."

"No, no. You were there. You saw everything too. Everything is your story, too."

"Ja, but Gerda will like to tell you. You can ask her when you see her. *Toch*, Marget." She winces, annoyed.

She turns away, wiping the bracelets of foam from her wrists. She stares up at the kitchen clock. Her face tightens. Now, she must be thinking, now they are taking my poor Gerda. Now they are putting my poor fellow under the knife.

"You need something?" She turns suddenly to me.

"No. I mean yes."

"Something for dessert? Something to drink?"

"No. No, thank you, Oma."

Well, that's it, then. I've done it. Or rather, I don't know how to do it. I don't know how to get her to stay, to sit up, to trust me. I don't know how to talk to her. I thought I knew. I thought I was getting an inkling about it, about her, but now she seems to be slipping away from me again. Now I'm tired, I'm sleepy. Maybe we just both come from a long line of weak, dozing women.

"I just thought it would be nice," I say dully, because it doesn't matter anymore, "to talk to you."

My grandmother lifts her head, surprised. Her eyes narrow, hard, into my face, as if she can't quite bring me into focus. As if I were only just outside the circle of her vision, hovering somewhere, very near the edge, but also near the edge of a very deep well. Then her face breaks out in a lovely smile.

"Ja!"

What's happened? She's plucking my t-shirt playfully at the shoulder. She's laughing, modestly, girlishly. What is it? What's come over her? And then I see it. Of course. Of course! I have flattered her. I've whispered to her, perhaps in words she hasn't heard for years, You are desirable, I want to be with you, you alone. My grandmother must be remembering it, the torturing, the sweet pleading: how someone else's longing can be like sugar melting on the tip of your tongue.

Her skin is coming to life again, her face is flushing.

I'll have to remember this.

Later, when we've settled into our places on the Danish loveseat, leaving Gerda's spot a soft hollow in the fabric between us, my grandmother relaxes and tries, simply, to talk. Her voice isn't very powerful; she mumbles. She halts and stumbles and trips over her own words, as if her own memories, the ruins of her old self, were stones blocking her path. Yet as she whispers and falters and coughs and begins again, I grow sharp, I watch her even more closely, I try to pick out the way for her. It's as if I'm wearing her eyes in my face.

How good it feels, after all, to slip away. How peaceful to submerge yourself in someone else's story. I understand, now, Mama. It's lovely to get lost in history. A person could get used to this way of being, I think: dreaming and still being awake.

❈ Chapter Thirteen ❈

During the monsoon the rains begin in the morning and end again in the evening, this is almost exactly as if the sky were a clock. The water slows to a drip, like this—tick tick tick—coming over the lips of our roof, and all around the house the ground takes on a soft shine, like a sore heel that has been turned over and bathed by the sky. Inside the house I stand waiting, and watching. We move slowly, the four of us, like oxen, behind the windows. Sometimes we toss like elephants, impatiently, waiting for all the weather and ticking to stop. We look up and down and back and forth across the lawn, across the grass, we fall into the rotting cane chairs, sighing, pulling the moldy blades out. Until the rain comes to a full stop, like a train. Then we can get up and go out through the porch, step onto the terrace, down into the courtyard, and out onto the grass. Gerda and Elly like their feet bare. They like to walk on the lawn, sinking in as they go. They leave a path of little foot-lakes behind them.

After the rain it is very quiet, cool, we have this ringing quiet in Java this way before nightfall. We start to work, picking the dripping blossoms off the kenanga trees. The kenanga crouch around the house here like green tigers wearing jewels. We take turns climbing up the bamboo ladder, filling the bowls we make of our skirts. We take both petals and whole flowers and pieces of smelly bark. When we are done we have the smell of the tree on us; we feel sticky, like a honeybee between the legs. In the kitchen, we throw everything into pots and watch the flowers boil. It was Pippy's idea to make the toilet water. We can sell it for money. To Japanese women who can still afford to smell delicious, who can get no more perfumes behind the blockade.

Pippy was our seller of the kenanga. We made her look more attractive, like for market. We gave her the nicest clothes we had left, and I fixed her heavy-cheeked face so she didn't look so much like a puppy. Then she was ready to go into the empty temple-houses of the Japanese.

Sometimes, Pippy told me, only the Malay maid would come to the door, sniffing at her. Sometimes the lady herself would come, whispering inside her long, rich sleeves. Her heart would be as cold and hidden as a pearl. Sometimes she will buy a bottle, Pip says, and sometimes not. Sometimes she will pay, and other times only promise later. No one likes the Japanese wives, the women of the officers and the profiteers. Pippy says

they are different from their husbands: the knives of
their voices are much shorter, and they carry them
higher in their throats.

When at first we heard the stories we tried not to believe them. Japanese soldiers hide black tails inside their
uniforms. Indonesian women who went near them disappeared like spirits from the face of the earth, going
mysteriously away at night by trucks and by boats.
Gerda brought these stories home to us at night along
with the shoes she had to clean. She cleaned them and
we sat watching and listening to her, our mouths open,
we don't want to believe her, but we do. She told us that
the soldiers have been to the hospital to visit the sick
children. That they brought them all candy and toys at
first, and then sent all the nurses away. When the nurses
were allowed to come back, an hour later, the beds were
empty and torn with bayonet scars. There is no telling
what they will do to us, Gerda says. We have to be careful, we should all stay near the house. We try to feel
warm in the dark night, close together around the light
of our illegal wireless.

I heard Queen Wilhelmina on a wireless. Speaking
to us in Indonesia, from the other side of the world. An
attack on Pearl Harbor, she told me then, is an attack on
the Dutch East Indies. The Queen is the mother of our
colony. Her voice sounded far away, but familiar, like
someone you know but never see.

She told me the Allies were coming to protect me,
and that the Japanese would be forced to retreat. That
the Americans and English would be coming in to roar

like a row of tigers in front of our beaches. But the Allies didn't protect me, or my husband, or my baby, and we heard later how they were all sunk or driven away. The Japanese are strong. They came to our city, and they took us like smashed fruits left on the ground.

Now I am all alone, with these three women, already a year behind the blockade. All the Americans and British can do for us now, Gerda says, is shut us in like meat with hungry vultures.

At first I keep a little to myself. Gerda and Pip and Elly are so kind. They give me food, and clothes, and blankets for my baby, and everything they have managed to hide in Gerda's house. I don't know why they help me. Gerda says it is because I am so pale. Her house is more beautiful than anything I have ever seen, beautiful as a church. It is so white it is like wading through the foam on a pond, and when you walk through the halls it's like pulling something beautiful behind you, the rooms are like a veil behind you, flowing.

Pippy could see that I was nervous at first, so she took me out and showed me the garden. She made me sit and rest under the trees by the pond and fanned me with her palm-leaf fan. I like the way Pippy's cheeks are like two ripe plums hanging in her face.

Elly is kind, but her eyes are wide apart. She is the sad one, always talking about the times before the war. She told me how she had had a little baby too, how it had died and how they buried it, in a yard beside the church.

She likes to pat my hand as if she is very old. She is only twenty-five. She takes me in the kitchen and shows me how to cook. I am learning their mother's recipes for nasi goreng and babi ketjap. Together Elly and I do the washing in the house, while Gerda and Pippy are working.

When Elly starts having nightmares, screaming that snakes are hiding in her bed, we decide we will all sleep together, in one big room. We put Frances's basket between the two beds, and in the night when she makes noises like a crying monkey, Gerda beside me reaches her thumb out for my baby to suck on.

Then I begin to see that we are all going to be like a family. Every one of us will be part of the family, and everyone will know what to do. I am the one who makes the others smile. I find music to play and dances to dance, and I cook the food and spread it in half-moons to make it beautiful on the plates. Pippy is the bargainer, she searches the streets, she brings us milk and old magazines and good, worn shoes. Gerda brings home money from the sugar factory, and the Japanese never find an error in her accounts. Elly plays and sings songs and teaches Frances about the *momok*, who will snatch her up in his arms if she ever goes outside the house. She teaches my baby an old Dutch play-song, galloping Frances on her lap and then dropping her and catching her low between the knees:

A farmer's horse, a farmer's horse

A lord's horse, a lord's horse

A lady's horse lady's horse lady's horse lady's horse

Hole in the road!

When I see my baby falling that way, I think about the days before I was married. I remember those years, I was three whole years alone, in the city, before he found me. No other Dutch boy danced so crazily then, to the music. No other Dutch boy wanted to marry me. I wore dresses that had sleeves like white butterfly wings. We were married even though no one from his family came. We went to live in an apartment with his money. When the Japanese came to take him I was already big with Frances, I was round like a dog, my hair was greasy. He turned in the door and shouted at me to go to the nuns. But after the baby was born the sisters sent me away again. No one told me how my baby would hurt me. No one said my baby would do so much kicking.

Sometimes the five of us in this house have nothing to eat except rice, but then we sit together and dream about the good, fat days before the war. About dried, sweetened tamarinds, and mangosteen, and fruity rudjak, and the hundred spices, and sweet mung bean cakes, and dark ketjap. Some days our stomachs roll like ships out at sea, ships that are lost far, far from land. And all we can do is sit eating dried fish, waiting for the rain to stop.

No one likes to look in the mirror because we are growing old. Everything is rotting, going green, brown, black. Our dresses are thinning into fishnets on our shoulders. The white-ant is getting into the house, eating the chairs.

When the dry season comes a second time, Gerda says, Now maybe the Japanese will go. But they only stick, harder, like black beetles. They are burning fields, building houses, temples. Another monsoon passes, and another. Gerda says even the water running in the canals now looks Japanese. Everyone bows to the officers' cars.

She was walking home one evening from the club when she met Dr. Mushiake. He said to her, "May I help you?"

Gerda told us how his long black auto pulled up beside her. She tried not to look at it, not to stare at him, hiding her face behind the bag of dirty shoes she was carrying.

"I've seen you at the club," the doctor said to her through the window. "Why don't you let me take you home?"

"*Arigato*," Gerda said, bowing and not looking at him. "I don't need."

"I know. But you'll ruin your feet walking that way."

"*Arigato*," she said. "No, thank you."

Dr. Mushiake pulled his car in front of her to stop her walking. Then he came out and opened the door.

"Please. You can trust me, *njonja besar*. I've seen you at the tennis club. I am Dr. Mushiake. You play so beautifully. I would be honored if you would let me take you home."

We couldn't believe Gerda when she told us we would be having dinner with a Japanese. Elly said she would stay in the house, she was scared of the *momok*, she wanted to stay behind with Frances. So the three of us waited outside in the dark for his car, and when it came the yellow beams swung on us like search lights. But inside he was smiling and beckoning to us, curling his finger.

The doctor's house was so beautiful, more beautiful, even, than Gerda's. Its walls were made of white paper. He had everything in it, the whole world sitting in his corners, Dutch and Indonesian, Chinese, Japanese, and American, stone, wood, glass, metal, and ivory. He told us he had lived in the Indies for twenty years, collecting everything he found, and liking everything. We saw the shadow of a woman move behind one of the paper walls.

"My wife speaks no English," the doctor said. He bowed to her as she came out. She was shaped like a pear. He told us they were expecting their first son later in the year. Mrs. Mushiake bowed to us, smiling.

"*Hajimemashite.*"

So this is how we had dinner, every Sunday, with a Japanese doctor and his wife. Every Sunday he picked us up in the darkness after curfew, hiding us on the floorboards, sneaking us through the back alleys to the gate of his house. We sat by the light of white candles, and ate raw eggs, cooked meat, and steamed vegetables. Gerda and Pippy and the doctor drank sake wine, while Mrs. Mushiake poured tea, holding the lid like a baby's forehead. Sometimes we laughed and made fun. Sometimes Gerda and the doctor drank too much, and then they argued about the place of the Dutch Indonesian.

"You should give up," said the doctor. "The Dutch don't care about you. Your place is with us now, with the future."

"I don't like your future," Gerda said. "I'm not fooled by you people."

"We're not fooling anyone! Isn't it better that Asians control Asia? At least we are relatives of the same family."

"You are not my family. Bah! Look at you. The Indonesians thought you would be better than the Dutch. Now look where they are, in the trenches, in the brothels, in their graves. I am not fooled."

"It is the Dutch who have fooled you. They never treated you with respect. Now you sit and wait for them to come back, like a woman who waits for a man who beats her."

"You don't know anything. You only see out of one eye. I see out of two, and I see better than you."

"You are cross-eyed, you mixed-bloods! You see nothing."

We changed the talk. Pippy smiled and pointed to Mrs. Mushiake's big stomach and held up twin fingers. Mrs. Mushiake blushed and covered her face with her fan. I tried to think of a signal to tell her not to be afraid.

One morning someone scratches like a bird on our front door. I go with Gerda to answer it, because she is afraid the *momok* will trick her and kidnap me from the back of the house.

"*Njonja besar?*"

It is a thin Malay boy, making his *semba*. Gerda whispers to me, It's all right, this is only my auto-boy, Rakijo.

"How are you, Rakijo?"

"*Njonja* keeps her husband's house well."

Gerda won't let Rakijo inside. He works for the Japanese, now. His mother is *kokkie* at a Japanese house, his father is *gardu* of the yard. "My parents are well," Rakijo says. "But they miss the old days. With *njonja* and her husband, before the war."

"Then you shouldn't have left us."

Rakijo bows and says nothing.

I am here but nobody sees me. Gerda doesn't see me. Rakijo doesn't see me. I am like a wall giving them shade, hiding them. They are looking down at their feet, their shoulders curled forward, like long grass that has bent too far to stand up again. Rakijo is taller than Gerda, but he is only a boy, and a Malay, and his *gardu* uniform is a dirty brown, lighter than his skin. He looks like a calf rolled in mud. I see he is trying to pile something between his toes. It keeps slipping away.

"*Njonja besar,*" he says. "You must listen to me now. They are coming to take your house. I have heard them in the house of my mother's master. They are coming because this house is too fine for you, and they say you are too proud. They say you like to win too much. They will come soon, *njonja,* maybe tomorrow, or the next day. Please, *njonja,* I am saying you must leave. *Njonja,* please to move from your husband's house."

He breathes fast. He is excited. I want to run into the house. I am afraid, I want Pippy and Elly to come and bring Frances, and I want us to run and hide in a hole. Gerda looks at Rakijo, like she doesn't believe him. Then she believes him. I know Gerda.

"Thank you, Rakijo. Thank you very much. You should go now. You should tell your family we thank them. You should tell them how good it was to see you."

"Yes, *njonja*. You will be going now?"

"Yes. We are going. Thank you, Rakijo."

"Njonja, do you still have the car I used to clean? Did they take it?"

"They took it, Rakijo."

"I am sorry, *njonja*."

"Good-bye, Rakijo."

"Good-bye, *njonja*."

That night we went to Dr. Mushiake's house. Elly and Frances came too. We sat on the floormats in the dark and no one was laughing. The doctor bowed his head to Gerda and said sadly, "They will only take what is best. I am afraid they are a little like me. They are collectors, also. But they are very new at it. Ambitious. They had nothing in Japan, they were nobodies when they were there. Now they are like poor people who dream they wake up in a room full of chickens. I can do nothing to help you—it is too dangerous for us both. Can you find someone, to give you a place to stay?"

That night Gerda sent a boy with a message to the Chinese *kampong*. In the morning we started taking the furniture out of the house and putting it on the drive.

I remember how very tired I am. I only have to lift the small chairs, the easy ones, but they feel so heavy, their feet are like chunks of earth. It takes all four of us to push Gerda's piano out; it leaves marks on the floor behind us, like black claws. Frances runs around us and in between our legs, holding onto the neck of her puppet. Gerda tells us to take down the curtains. We take out the carpets. We bury her pictures, her money. When we are finished, there is almost nothing left inside the house, only pots and the mattresses from our beds. Gerda stands outside looking at the roof—maybe we can take that down, too.

We sit on top of the furniture, waiting. Finally an old Chinese comes slowly up our street, with his cart and oxen.

"Can you take all of this?" Gerda asks him.

"Yes, *njonja besar*. Of course. Tell me what you would like me to do with it."

"Take it away. You can keep it. It is yours."

"Your husband would not like that, *njonja besar*. Let me sell it, and I'll give you the money."

"My husband is dead. I can't sell it. I want you to have it. You helped my husband to make it. Now I can't keep it in my house."

The old Chinese man looked down. He had a boy next to him in the cart. The boy was in disguise, dressed like a girl.

"*Njonja* does not want the pieces sold?"

"No. I don't want."

"I see. I have brought my grandson. They have taken my son for the fields."

I am still so very tired as we lift everything into the cart. Then it starts to rain. When we are finished the night is so dark the legs of the chairs look like the horns of demons, fighting each other. The old man and his

grandson turn the cart away, not looking back at us, rid-
ing toward the *kampong*. Elly and Pippy are crying,
watching them go. But Gerda says we aren't finished.
We don't go to sleep until we've smeared mud on all the
walls and floors and doors of the house. Then we go to
sleep in a room smelling of worms, in a house that looks
like the inside of a broken pot.

In the morning we stand outside while the Japanese
go through the house. We wait under the trees, looking
down at our feet. An officer comes out holding his nose
like a purse. Indo pig! he says to Gerda. His tires spit
mud on us.

Look at that! Gerda says. Look at that! They are nervous! They are hurrying! This is a good sign. This is
something new. Soon the Allies will be coming. Soon,
soon, you will see.

We listen that night to the wireless. I keep Frances on
my lap, letting her fall asleep to the voices. We are like
five beggars around a small fire. We are at the beginning
of 1945.

Dr. Mushiake sent us a letter saying that he and his wife
were leaving. He was taking her out, now, to Jakarta,
while there was still time, so that his son could be born
safely in a hospital. His letter was full of respect for
Gerda. I have been honored, he said. He told Gerda, You
must be careful. You must be aware, he wrote to us,
nothing can ever be the same. Never can we look each
other in the eyes. With the letter he sent his best sake

wine, and also a silver photo of himself with Mrs. Mushiake.

After Dr. Mushiake left, Pippy came home running to tell us what she saw. A Japanese soldier, walking, with glass eyes like a dead animal. Another soldier, with his boots tied around his neck like two stones.

It's all right, Gerda said. But no one can believe in the bombs. No one can believe we felt nothing. I asked Gerda, Why didn't I feel anything? I feel everything. But I felt nothing under my feet, from something so huge.

No one moved for a long time then, and nothing happened. No one breathed. No one made a sound.

Gerda won't go to the sugar factory anymore. Or to play tennis. Pippy stays inside and makes Frances stay away from the windows. Maybe we should all stay away from the windows, Gerda whispers.

We break them, at night, to make the house look more empty. We don't use light. We stay hidden. We are like pale fish trying to hide on a dark, slippery bottom.

Before the Japanese are even gone we begin hearing the voices on the radio.

Kill them. Kill the filthy colonials. Kill them.

Where is the Queen now, to save us? The Javanese want no more Dutch blood in Indonesia. Listen, Gerda says. If you pull a knife out, then of course the wound will bleed. They are remembering not the Japanese sword, but the Dutch one.

I want us to run, to hide in a hole, but I don't know where.

We stay low in the empty-looking house. Sometimes when I sleep I dream of Rollie's beautiful furniture, going away, ruined in the rain.

Gerda listens to the voices on the wireless. Maybe the church will take us, she says, whispering, if we have to go. They will have to take us.

On the night the fighting began she made us cover our bodies with the mattresses. But Gerda stood by the window, uncovered, watching everything. I could see her in the flashes of light. I could hear the planes, and the sounds of something screaming falling, and what sounded like people in the dark. Gerda was shaking her fists. Fight now, she shouted, you fight, you fight!

After the Battle of Surabaya it was so quiet we thought our eardrums were broken. But still we heard the voices on the radio:

Kill them. Kill them. Kill them.

Maybe we will be strong enough to run, Gerda says. If we rest, maybe we will be ready. But we have nothing to eat. We have no rice, no milk. My daughter's eyes are like two black empty pots in her face. Elly's mind has left its house and is sitting in her hands. She sits with Frances on the floor and makes shadows with the *wayang* puppet on the wall. Sometimes we all sit and stare at the shadows, and if a lizard runs across them, our mouths turn to water. But it's bad luck to kill a *tjit-jak*. So we try pulling grass from the yard instead. Look at this green grass soup! we say to Frances. Look, look, look at it! It's so good!

Green soup will make your eyes green. Green grass will make you grow.

After a while I don't feel it. I don't feel hungry any-more. I feel I'm floating on my back: I'm on the back of a giant snake that is my hunger. I'm only swimming on the back of my hunger, it's only twisting and turning underneath me. When I'm asleep I'm still awake be-cause of its turning, and when I'm awake I'm asleep because the waves are so soft. We are all awake now, all night long. I am crazy, Pip says. I can smell rice and eggs cooking. I can smell fish, Elly says. Me too, says Gerda. We can all smell rice and fish and cooked eggs. We are all going crazy, we can even hear a knocking at the back door. We can imagine Gerda getting up and floating away toward it in the moonlight, and then coming back to us with a bowl. We are so crazy we can do nothing except put our faces in it.

We say nothing until everyone is finished. No one is ashamed, no one is embarrassed. We are licking our fingers and scraping the bowl and sticking grains of rice onto our thumbs and eating them before Gerda can tell us.

She didn't know what would happen to her, she said, when she went to the door. She didn't care. She was so crazy she wanted to see who was waiting there to kill her. When she saw it was only one small man, she took a deep breath, ready to hit him. Then he held some-thing out to her.

He was an Indonesian. She didn't know him. She looked in his eye. He said one word to her: silver. Gerda told him she would have some tomorrow. He looked as if he didn't believe her. He looked as if he wasn't going to give her the bowl. Then Gerda looked in his eye again, and he knew he would have to come back. He gave the bowl to her and went into the dark.

Now, Gerda said, we'll see.

We gave him some of Gerda's silver, every night. Every night he took away an empty bowl and handed her back a full one. Every night he slipped away through the moonlight like a man shamed by visiting a paid woman.

When we have eaten we listen to the radio. Dutch nationals are advised to report to refugee camps. But how? Gerda says. We are on the wrong side of the city.

In the night we hear again a man's tapping on the door. Our stomachs are growling like tigers, waiting for him. Gerda starts to get up. Before she can leave we hear a high voice whispering:

"*Njonja! Njonja!* You must go! They have seen your light! *Njonja*, someone has seen it, your little light, someone has seen the little red light from your radio! *Njonja*, you must hurry! They are coming now, you must leave! *Njonja*, please hurry, now, please, please go!"

Gerda pulls me up. "*Kom snel!*" she hisses. She takes our papers. "*Weg wezen! Weg wezen!*"

Rakijo's feet are still running in the dark ahead of us. Gerda is running in the dark, shouting at us, she is carrying Frances, and Pip is pulling Elly along, and I am running, running, we are all running, as fast as we can, but the house is still so close behind us I can hear when they break in more windows. I can hear gunshots, until finally they are only the sounds of stones cracking under our shoes. And now finally we are far enough away so that no one can hear us, no one can see us. Rakijo is gone and we are all alone, together, crouching under a Japanese hedge.

Then we get up and start walking in the dark to the British camp. We crawl in the shadows near the *kampong*, staying low. If we can get inside, Gerda says, they will have to take us with them. They will have to take us. We are women and children.

I don't know how far we walk. Many hours. I am jumping at every sound. Everything in the streets is dark. When we get to the British camp, Gerda stops us. We can't ask them, she says. What if they say no? We're Indonesian, Dutch. Not British. She finds a place where we can climb, unseen, over the fence.

I will carry Frances, she says. You go first. Hurry, hurry.

Pip and Elly go up into the trees, fast as monkeys. They jump to the other side.

Now you, Fan.

I go up and then I feel Pippy's and Elly's arms catching me, and the ground under my feet hard and steady.

Here I come, whispers Gerda.

I can see her face at the top of the tree. I see Frances, holding her around the throat. Then the branches collapse.

We catch them and we fall down underneath them and hold Frances and cover her mouth, not moving, lying all together. I don't how long we lay still there. I remember the sky looked very naked, that night.

Chapter Fourteen

"Wﾍhat—?"

"It's the phone, Oma. I'll get it."

My foot's asleep, but that's not the worst of it. My head has that clogged, terrible feeling you get when you doze in the middle of the day, when you know you've done something you shouldn't have and your brain begins paying you back for it. I stumble to the counter and manage to pick up the phone by the fourth ring, but the woman's voice at the other end sounds like it's coming from far away. I hear a hum in my head like a battery charging. My voice sounds strange in my ears.

"I'm sorry? What did you say?"

"It's the hospital. I need to speak to Mrs. Bischop."

"It's okay, you can tell me, I'm her granddaughter."

"No, I need to speak to her directly."

"Please, it's all right. She can't come to the phone right now. She's asleep. She's not—feeling well."

I look over at Fan. She's still in several pieces on the loveseat, waking up. She looks toward me with vague eyes, squinting over her nose as if it were somebody else's in her way.

"It's for you, Oma. It's okay," I say into the receiver. "She's right here."

"I really think it's best I let her know."

"They want to talk to you, Oma."

Fan shakes her head at me.

"No, she doesn't want to. She's tired. I'm sure I can give her the message." If I were more alert I might be getting angry.

"It's about Mrs. Van Doorn."

"Yes, I know. Is she ready now?"

"The surgery took longer than they expected. She's just now getting into recovery. The doctor says you should probably wait at least another two hours before you come in here."

"Is everything okay?"

"Our older patients have a harder time coming out of things. They're awake, but they're not themselves. It takes some time. We don't want them to feel pressured."

"But everything should be okay? Later on."

"Of course."

"How long did you say?"

"About three o'clock."

Fanny is looking more composed now. She only winces a little when I sit down beside her.

"That was the nurse."

"Ja?" Her eyes grow wide. She's only just remembered the operation, and looks at me as if I'm terrible, as if I've just brought a terrible, remembered curse into her house.

"*Alles is goed.*" I hug her.

"*Alles is goed,*" she repeats, nodding. It sounds like she's trying the words out. Then her eyes fill from the bottom like two cups.

We say hardly anything on the drive over to the hospital. Fan has brought some of her nasi goreng in a small bowl to give to Gerda. I don't know how the hospital will feel about the spicy food, so I've had my grandmother hide it in a paper bag. If I get a chance, I can talk to the nurses and tell them what it is and how much salt is in it. Fan clutches the bag on her lap, looking secretive, withdrawn. Now I have to wonder if she'll ever talk so much again. Maybe I've drained her, put too much pressure on her memory chords. I take my foot off the gas, slowing and wheeling us into the parking lot. Fanny rocks sideways, bending. She's changed her sweater and the new blouse clings to her bird-like chest, thinly, sweatily.

Gerda is sitting up in her bed, her right knee bandaged, I can't help but notice, to the thickness of a small child.

"Ja, ja," she says groggily as Fan stoops to kiss her. She pulls away when my grandmother tries to whimper something in her ear. "Ja. Stop. Everything is okay now."

"Hey Gerda. How're you feeling?"

"Not so bad. A little funny. How was this one?"

"Fine. Are you okay?"

"Ja, ja," she says vaguely, reaching to push something invisible out of her way. An IV needle is taped to the back of her wrist. It makes her strong hand look fragile, like an animal with an injured back.

"I can't see you there. I need my glasses."

"Here."

"Better. Fan, you sit down. Marget, you can sit on the bed." Like Napoleon arranging his island.

"Well? Tell us what the anesthesia felt like."

"Bah. I don't remember anything. Only bright lights over me, turning, how you say it, like a helicopter. Whish whish. And then they make me count backwards, one hundred, ninety-nine, ninety-eight. It's stupid! Why do they make me start so high? Of course I couldn't finish."

"You're still a little bit fuzzy."

"I'm not fuzzy, I'm thirsty. They are so slow around here. Where is my juice? I'm ready already to leave."

"Not for three days."

"Bah, I go crazy in here in three days."

"Does anything hurt?"

Gerda looks at Fan first. Then she looks back at me, shaking her head carefully, as if there are tiny bells inside it she doesn't want disturbed. "Not yet. Only this." She points to the IV. "But they say I will have pain, later."

"That's good." At least that's what Mama used to tell me. "It means you're healing."

"Ja. You know what I should really like, *kind?*"

"What?"

"I should like to watch, next time. For my other knee. I like to stay awake. Do you know, they can give you something in your spine? The ep-i-du-ral. You know it?"

"I think they give it to women having babies."

"I don't know about that. But I like to have a chance, next time. I should like to watch what the doctor is doing. Ja! That would be interesting, to see the inside of your body. I like blood and muscles. I think I should love my bones. Wouldn't you like to see it?"

"Maybe you can, next time."

"*Nee,* I don't think so. My doctor says I'm too old. Why can't I go home, *kind?*"

"Therapy, remember?"

"Therapy?"

"To make your knee strong again."

"Oh, that's right."

Fanny says nothing. But she never takes her eyes off Gerda, like a distant cloud that won't take its eye off a mountain. We sit together until Gerda's face starts drooping, until her chin starts to waver toward the chest of her hospital gown. She wakes up and tries to pretend she's looking for something she's dropped down inside it. "We'd better go, you're getting sleepy," I say.

"Ja, okay."

Fanny is wide awake and can even hold her head up, calmly, as we walk out the door. It's something new, watching my grandmothers trade places this way. One eye brighter when the other one is dark. One flying

154

higher when the other one is low. Fanny's thin, pale body is the brighter, at the moment: as I guide her toward the elevators I might as well be carrying a flickering candle down the hallway.

By the time Tante Pip calls to check up on us, I can't explain exactly what's happened.

"It's weird, Tante. Fan's moving things. She's going through everything. She's throwing things out and she's giving me things I don't need to take back with me. She's going through all her closets and taking everything out and setting some things aside and putting everything else back again. She's cleaning out everything. I try to get her to sit down, but she won't even rest for a minute. And Corinne said I need to be watching out for her heart, but I can't make her stop. She just waits until I'm not looking. Then she's up on a chair trying to get to the top of some cabinet. I can't figure out what to do. Gerda's coming back, in two days. . . . No, Fan's going to make them a cot downstairs so they don't have to climb upstairs. I'm getting up earlier just so I can see what she's getting into. She hardly sleeps now. She acts likes there's something hiding somewhere. She's washing everything inside and out. She's making me tired."

Tante Pip's voice is crooning, soothing. "Ja, don't worry. I will take care of them when I come."

Pip is a person who won't be hurried—so I know, in spite of everything I've said, she won't be coming down any sooner than she's planned. She tries to put Corinne on the line, but my aunt only shouts hello and a mild obscenity from the background. It's a sign. It's not that Corinne doesn't want to talk to me. It's that she doesn't want Gerda to know she did, that she cared enough to come on the line. She must be even madder than I thought.

Now Fan is compulsively dusting and redusting, as if every speck and mote must be located, isolated, captured, gloated over, and then expelled from the house. After I've dusted every one of the brass candlesticks on the mantelpiece she comes along with a cloth and dusts them again. She still doesn't trust me. I wipe the back of the brass *tjitjak*. She comes and wipes it off again. It feels like a dance, a set of intricate variations for two. We vacuum the living room twice. Her neck shines faintly under her powder. I'm the one who's getting dizzy, tired, the one who finally has to go up to her room and hold her head between her knees and lie down. When I wake up Fanny is in the kitchen again, cleaning out another one of her drawers.

She must have been going through another cabinet somewhere, because sitting on the counter is a clutch of china cups, eggshell thin, resting one inside the other.

"Look." Fan pulls me by the arm. "You take these."

"No more, Oma. Please."

"You can."

"I can't!"

There's already the hoard she's left in my room, things she apparently can't bear to let go of, and so is pushing, stubbornly, onto me. Old shawls, slippers, and bathrobes. Faded linens and pillowcases, extra towels, almost-new milk pitchers, Tupperware, glass bottles, napkin rings, as if she's decided I should be setting up house. Here, she keeps saying. Here and here. Take more, take more. While all the while her own house is growing cleaner, lighter, brighter. She's getting ready. As if for a bride.

"They're too fragile, Oma. I'll never get them back in one piece."

She frowns. Her lips pout out. "But we bring them from Holland. They were your mama's."

"That's what I'm saying. They look antique. You wouldn't want something to happen to them now."

She looks me up and down. Hard. "I don't worry. You take them. I don't want it."

She's like trying to fight a flock of pigeons with my hands tied behind my back. I can hear her, late at night, muttering, fluttering, going through her bedroom drawers, one by one. Taking things out, folding them back in. Carefully. No accountant reviewing her columns could be more meticulous.

The last touch comes the day before Gerda comes home. We set the two cots I got down from the attic in the space where the coffee table stood, in front of the television. After trying them different ways, Fan has me push the loveseat aside and arrange the cots at right angles to each other, so Gerda will be able to get out on both sides. Their heads will lie close together, at the intersection. She takes more care in arranging these beds than anything she has fidgeted over the last two days. The pillowcases are crisp, the white sheets pulled taut. I half expect her to stand at attention and bounce a coin off them. Then I notice how the living room has been quietly transformed: it looks like a camp, clean and comforting. Fan doesn't want to go with me when I pick Gerda up at the hospital. She wants to wait here, a welcoming party, a surprise.

When Gerda finally totters in it's like seeing a child light up, almost afraid. Her eyes grow round. Fanny blushes. "Ja," Gerda blinks, nodding, wheeling her metal walker forward. "Ja. This is good, Fan."

Everything seems to be all right, everything seems to be falling into place again. On the drive home Gerda had had me worried. She was touchy, embarrassed, irritated by the fact that she needs a rolling set of four legs, for now, instead of one cane. She snapped at me for driving too fast, too slow, looked out the window enviously at passersby, with the unforgiving frown of an amputee. I reminded her she'd be getting more therapy; the hospital would be sending someone over to the house. Gerda snorted at me, unimpressed. Poor Gerda. Reduced to a half-woman. Floundering like a mermaid on the shore.

She rolls the walker, awkwardly, over the carpet to her cot, and tries sitting down with her bulky knee. Her lips go white. The knee sticks straight out in front of her, like something prehistoric. Fanny comes to life. She's brought candies and magazines and furred slippers and Gerda's cane. Gerda waves my grandmother impatiently off, her face growing suddenly cloudy.

"*Laat maar*, now! Go away!"

I start moving Fan strategically toward the kitchen. "Why don't you make Gerda some coffee, Oma? I'm sure she's missed it."

"I don't want anything! Just leave me alone, you two. Why are you always crowding? A person can't breathe."

"Let's go, Oma. Let's go."

In the kitchen it's my grandmother's turn to look wide-eyed, afraid. "It's okay, Oma. We just have to let her be, for a while."

"*Waarom?*"

"She needs the rest."

We hide for an hour, busying ourselves peeling and chopping vegetables. Of course I should have seen this coming. Gerda is helpless. Gerda is hating it. Gerda will rail against being the weak one in the house, against having to have Fan do everything for her. Gerda will have to roll around in front of us like a circus bear on her hind legs. Gerda will be unable to smell her roses. Gerda is immobile. Gerda is unarmed.

My grandmother is listening for something, her head cocked. A tone, a signal, something suggestive, coming from the quiet living room. Eventually she must hear it, because she picks up the coffee tray and carries it out formally, as if Gerda were the Queen herself.

Gerda says nothing. My grandmother and I sit down, cautiously. Gerda is watching television, but without the volume.

"Bah." She changes the channels with the remote. "There is nothing on. Only game shows and dirty movies."

The stations click by, colorfully. They remind me, for some reason, of the wings being torn off of insects. Gerda *hmph*s at the screen. Dirty movies, for my grandmothers, are anything that shows passionate kissing, or worse. Even brief glimpses of bedroom scenes leave them squirming, as if they've been--p caught in the middle of an orgy. Even now their hands sit lightly in their laps, ready to fly up to their faces. "You have anything you like to watch?" Gerda snaps.

"*Jeopardy?*"

"That's too hard."

When she starts to doze from the heaviness of her painkillers, I nudge Fan and whisper that I'm going upstairs. Fanny nods, but her eyes are trapped-looking. I don't think she wants to be left alone with her.

Gerda opens one eye. She grunts at me. "Where are you going?"

"See you later." I kiss her. "I'm going to bed."

"Uh," she grunts back. "Too young."

Upstairs is darkness, emptiness. No light spreads out from under their closed bedroom door, lighting my way in the hallway. Instead I am alone. I see nothing, I hear nothing, only a vague scuffling downstairs, under the thin floor under my feet, a tossing, a tussling, an arguing, what sounds like a rearranging. Fan! Gerda calls out abruptly, as if waking up from a bad dream. You didn't put a light down here! You forgot to put out a night light!

I will do it tomorrow, Fan soothes her in Dutch. I will do it first thing in the morning.

Then everything goes quiet, nothing moves. Only the slow rhythm of the night, undulating.

Chapter Fifteen

Fanny and Gerda are fighting.

I've never seen anything like it. They aren't speaking to each other. Or, when they do, it's like each of them is standing up briefly to hurl hot coals over a low barricade. Invisible weapons are flying through the house. Things hurtle, and nobody has touched them. My grandmothers are hardly able to handle their own words.

"Stupid!" Gerda shouts.

"Crazy!" Fanny whimpers.

In front of me they put up blank sheets for faces, hanging wrinkled. But I can hear them, when they forget they're not alone. Gerda wants her coffee before it's ready. Fanny won't bring it. Fanny brings down clothes she knows Gerda won't like. They ignore each other, they make low, dirty noises, like children. They try to push each other without seeming to try. If Gerda notices the black circles that are pooling around my grandmother's eyes, she makes no sign of it. Fanny won't give in. She cringes, but she doesn't cry out. It's as if she's found something she doesn't want to let go of, and she wants Gerda to see it, to hear it. She doesn't retreat behind the white flank of her face. She is frightened, she's uncertain. But she isn't mute.

"Stupid!" Gerda cries out.

"Crazy!" Fan whispers back.

What happened last night, when I wasn't watching them?

When Tante Pip arrives, honking her horn twice in the driveway, it's Fanny who's the first one out the door to see her, half running, half dragging herself across the yard. I come out in time to see my poor grandmother dropped like a wounded sparrow onto my great-aunt's big shoulder.

"*Toch!*" Tante says. "This is too much." Then she sees me, smiles. "*Dag*, Marget!"

She stands beside her huge, pearly-white 1960 Impala. Tante Pip looks like an astronaut landed abruptly on earth, in an old gray dress with a circular collar. Her packed and overflowing purse loops awkwardly over her arm, as if she's encumbered with equipment she isn't used to carrying. Her dyed hair is caught up under a black hairnet.

The car door is still open behind her, and I can see her pristine white vinyl seats, covered in clear plastic protectors. They're littered with a few stray gambling chips, and with the wrappings of brandy-liqueured candies. It's a long drive down from Reno.

"Skinny girl." Pip has unpinned Fan from her chest, and is hugging me. She has two beetled black hairs on her chin that poke. Her neck smells of licorice and cold sweat and cigarettes—probably Corinne's. She hands over her car keys. "Can you get my suitcase out of the trunk, please?"

No sooner have I pulled the bag out than she's lifting it out of my hands, changing her mind. "But aren't you tired, Tante?"

"You look more."

We go inside. Fanny starts pouring out a little stream of Dutch complaints into Pip's ear. Tante grunts. When we're in the living room, in front of Gerda and her white leg, Pip pulls up short, as if taken aback by what she sees.

Gerda acts surprised too.

"*Dag*, Dik?" Pip bends suddenly and smoothly down, kissing Gerda's slack cheek.

"*Dag*, Pip." Gerda frowns, kissing her back. Her eyes move suspiciously between Pip and Fan.

"Move over on this bed-thing, ja," Pip says. "I like to watch this program, too."

The woman in the toothpaste commercial is simply smacking her pearly white teeth.

"Marget." She looks up. "Why don't you and Fan go make us something to eat in there? I'm starving, really. Oh, this is a good picture," she returns to Gerda.

"Ja," Gerda nods.

"I don't get such a good picture at home."

"You have a bad set."

"It's old."

"Then you should get a new one."

"New one costs money," Pip says. "And it takes time."

"What, time?"

"You have to learn all the new buttons."

"*Nee,* the buttons are always the same."

"*Nee,* they change. Sometimes you have to start pushing in a different place."

"What different place?"

"Sometimes things change. Oh, you're so stupid! You're crazy. You don't know anything."

Then Fanny does something I've never seen her do. She pulls the sliding kitchen door out of its pocket in the wall, and closes them in. All I can hear now is the water she's running for rice. She hasn't even asked Tante if she wants it steamed or brown.

"*Alles is goed,* now," Pip says, sliding the pocket door closed again behind her. "Gerda is taking a nap."

My tante squeezes her bulk next to me behind the kitchen table. "She's crazy, you know," she says, nudging me. "She tells me if I don't leave her alone and keep quiet, she's not going to do my taxes next year. So what can I do? Of course I have to go! Sit down, Fan, you too. You rest now. We'll eat when Gerda wakes up."

My grandmother sits down, suddenly deflated.

"Well, Marget." Tante turns to me. "It's been so long now."

"A couple of years. Sorry."

"*Nee!* It's okay. You're so busy. Such hard work. Let me see your feet there. *Toch!* It looks like it hurts!"

"It doesn't, though."

"You're crazy! Maybe something like that should hurt. What do you hear from your mama, lately?"

I haven't actually. None of us has. It's one reason Gerda is so angry.

"Well, ja, I know, she's in Europe. Maybe it's because of the time difference, hey? But I don't think it's nice for her, not to come home right now."

"Pip!" Fan pipes up weakly. She's defending my mother. Like a hen that's been roused. Her neck has turned faintly red, territorial.

"Ja, ja. Well, here we have Marget anyway, in her place. Say, Marget, you like to ask me something?"

"What?"

"I don't know. Gerda says you are liking to ask a lot of questions these days."

So what else were they talking about in there?

"Go ahead, ask me something!" Pip pokes me, grinning. She lifts her double chin, proudly. "I remember things better than any of these old ones! I remember everything. These two, they were always too busy with each other. In the middle of a war!"

"Pip!"

Fanny says something to her in Dutch.

"Ja, ja! You didn't tell her that? Then I can. You like to hear, Marget, how we got out of Indonesia, at the end? It's a good story!"

"Sure, Tante. Go ahead."

"Okay, okay. So listen now, good. Because I go fast, when I talk, so I don't leave many things out. It goes like this. When we first have to leave from our house, because of the Indonesians, you know, we get to this British camp where Gerda takes us, and nobody even asks us what we are doing in there. Did you tell her, Fan? Ja, that's right. Nobody even cares how we got inside. Nobody even looks at us. Because everybody is much, much too afraid for themselves. There were so many people in that camp, you see. Women and many children, hungry, very hungry, even starving, and not all of them British, and some of them men who had been prisoners, who looked like ghosts, they look to me like bones some dogs have already eaten.

"Right away we start thinking, Elly and me—maybe we should try to look for our husbands. We think maybe they'll be there, because there are others, so many of them, and because we don't know then our husbands are already dead, killed by the Japanese. So of course we start looking. But then that camp was so crowded, with so many women looking for their dead husbands. They put us in lines for everything, for putting names down, for husbands, for food, for papers, sometimes for nothing at all. Gerda makes sure that we stand at the front of those lines. She says, If you wait and are good and you stay in the back, you will get nowhere fast. So for three days we stand in different lines. And for all that time the British were busy trying to get us out of our country. They were talking to the Indonesians, you see, trying to bargain with them, to barter, to let us go safely to the port. Because if they don't, then we are all food for komodos. They have already been killing some whites and half-whites in our city.

"So finally, we hear over the radio that the Indonesians are saying we can go. We are so happy. The British, they decide they are going to put us up in trucks, and these trucks will take us down to the ship. Only later, I think: Why do the Indonesians tell everyone on the radio where the British exactly are taking us?

"So the ship, the British told us, was ready. It was going to take us away from Surabaya, to Singapore. You can't imagine what that felt like, Marget, hearing that name, Singapore. We are so sad because we know we are leaving. We are so happy, because we know we are going to live. But if Indonesia is the only home you ever know, until then, your whole life——? I knew I had to give up my whole life, right then, Marget. That is what the Indonesians wanted from me.

"And so the trucks came. And now we see it—now we see it is really going to matter that we are only half-whites. We are at the front of the lines, just like Gerda said. But they make all us coloreds step aside and go to the back, and they let all the white British and Dutch go up first. You should have seen those people, Marget! Shouting and pushing and shoving. Pushing and fighting to get on that truck, climbing inside it like chickens. Until they are all standing in the back of it, shoved together. And then that truck goes, and do you know what? No one ever sees those people again. Later we found out why. We heard that truck was caught and turned over by mobs in the streets. We didn't know that then, we were only waiting. For the next truck, everyone white and brown is pushing and shoving again. Still the soldiers will not let those of us in the back move. This truck had more soldiers, I remember, with guns, so they must have known by then what happened to the other one. Those people only got rotten eggs thrown in their faces. We saw them later, still trying to wipe them off.

"Now those of us in the back, with the third truck, we can finally go. We are sweating, I can tell you that. At first we didn't think they would let us leave. They kept us waiting. An officer stood up in front of us and told us what to do. Don't look at anyone, he shouted. Don't open your mouths. Don't raise your heads. Don't take your eyes off the floor. Remember you will be endangering your lives.

"Do you remember that, Fan? How they made the little children sit on our feet. And Frances wasn't crying at all, it was almost like she was going to sleep. I don't think she remembers any of it. I remember everything, standing in there, and all the people close together around me, and some of us peeing in our pants. We smelled terrible. When we drove outside you could hear all the voices shouting—you could hear all those people waiting down in the lower streets, waiting to throw insults and eggs at us. But I didn't care. After that, I wasn't afraid. I just looked down. I just let them throw their things on top of me. That's what happens at the end of a war, Marget. Nobody moved, and none of us said anything, while these people shouted terrible things at us and threw their rotten vegetables. And finally we came to the port, and it was like coming out of a hole and into the sky. They had a big aircraft carrier waiting for us. And when we got on, it was so high up, the sea looked just like a big blue flag lying down. It looked just like a big Dutch flag lying down.

"The Americans took us to Singapore, and they left us there. We spent almost a year in that refugee camp before they finally sent us back to Holland. That camp wasn't so bad, hey, Fan? We lived in a little barracks, with little cots, very nice. We hung sheets up in between the families, to keep us private. Fanny had a little room and a cot with Gerda, and I had a little room with Elly. Remember? It wasn't so bad. You could have anything you wanted, in that camp. Magazines and chocolate and photos. If you could pay for them. Then the Dutch government sent us some money, to help. A kind of apology, you see, for not being able to keep the country where we were born. But Gerda, she just laughed when she saw that little money. She went away and she came back with a phonograph, and she had also a record that she bought from a Singapore man in the street. 'Who's Sorry Now,' it was called. You should have seen Gerda laugh when she played that song! 'Who's sorry now,' it goes. 'Who's sorry now.'"

My grandmother leans over, whispers something in Pip's ear.

"Ja, well, if she has to take the pills now, just go and give them to her."

My grandmother gets up, bravely. We wait for her to slide the door closed again, sealing it like the entrance to a cave.

"You're so quiet, Marget. What are you thinking?"

"Nothing, Tante. Just listening to you. And resting."

"But what are you resting from?"

She looks at me with her kind Buddha's face, plump with soft hairs.

"Can you keep a secret, Tante?"

"I think so."

"I quit dancing. I haven't told Gerda or Fan yet."

For a moment her look is like something broken against a wall. Surprised.

"*Nee*, Marget! Why did you do that?"

"Well—it's complicated."

"Ah. I see. You don't like to say it. But that's too bad. Why did you do it? You have a talent, like them, just like them. Why do you want to give it away?"

"Mama and Fan stopped dancing."

"Ja. Well. That's true."

She fidgets, trying, I suppose, to make the connection.

"You haven't told them yet?"

"I didn't think now would be such a good time."

"Well, that's good. It's nice you think of them first. So when did you decide this thing?"

"Not too long ago."

"Do you know what you're going to do, when you're not dancing?"

"I'm not sure. I'd like to study. Something. I like books. Mom and Dad said they'd help me, if I ever wanted to."

"That's like a whole new life for you."

"I know."

Tante watches me. Her thoughts seem to slide back into her face, behind the skin of her eyes, momentarily. Then she comes out, like a lizard, swinging her gaze forward and toward me again.

"But Fanny used to dance! I like it, Marget. She used to dance for us, in Indonesia, during the war. And in Holland. You never saw her then, Marget, but she could move in such a beautiful way. It made you think of something—delicious. Fan always made me think of something so beautiful."

"I wish I could have seen her do something."

"You're going to make her sad."

"I don't mean to."

"Ja," she shrugs. "Well. Maybe it's not so important. We have seen, in our lives, many things. No, it's not so bad. I wouldn't worry. Have you told your mother yet?"

"Not yet."

"So it's a real secret you're telling me."

"I told you so."

She looks hard at me.

"You like it, having your mama so far away?"

"No. Of course not."

"But you understand it?"

"I think so. I think you have to live your own life, someday. I think it's hard."

"I live my own life."

"I know you do. In Reno."

"Ja . . . you should come see me," she says vaguely. "Me and Corinne."

172

"I do like seeing you, Tante."

"Ja?" Her face brightens now, just as Fan's did when I told her I wanted to talk to her. With just the same surprise, wonder, pleasure. I wonder if there really are only a few true expressions in the world. And we're all simply passing them around, handing them off, when we don't need them. Putting them on like still-warm masks.

Or maybe it's a family resemblance.

"I'm afraid to tell Oma, Tante. I don't think she feels so good right now."

"*Nee,* you don't worry about Fan. She's okay. She makes hard decisions in her life, too."

"When?" I cast my mind back. Until recently, I can't remember Fan ever doing anything decisive.

"When she told her husband she wasn't going back with him."

"Oh, you mean in Holland."

"No! In Singapore. In that camp I was telling you about. Didn't I tell you that part, about Fan?"

"What?"

Pip stares as if we've both just walked into the room. "Didn't I tell you about Han?"

Tante Pip goes on with her story. She starts in the middle, and finishes it. She tells me about my grandfather, how he came to the camp, out of nowhere. How he showed up haggard and thin at the Singapore refugee center with a Red Cross list clutched in his hand. Fan's and my mother's names were on it. She tells me how she and Gerda and Elly watched from a distance, while Fan and my mother went out, shyly, to meet him. How

Gerda had watched nervously from behind a dormitory while my grandmother avoided her husband's arms, handing my mother into them, letting him hold the baby while they talked to each other. How my grandfather kept staring over and over again into their faces. My mother had cried, wriggling, struggling, in the arms of a stranger. Then Fanny had pulled her daughter away from him, and stepped back, and slowly begun saying the words no one had told her to say. That she had fallen in love with someone else. That she was not going to go back with him, that she was staying, in Singapore, with a person whose name was Gerda. That she was sorry for all his years in the prison camps, very sorry he had come all this way to find them. My aunt told me how my grandfather's face had gone white, like a mask. How his thin bones had crumpled as if he'd been struck, how he went away, a man with no pride, no family, no country. I feel sorry for my grandfather, watching him, seeing him slink away beaten that morning. But it's my grandmother. It's my grandmother I keep looking at. It's my grandmother I can't tear my eyes away from, who holds my gaze fast like a fist.

Mama lied to me. Or maybe she just couldn't tell me. Maybe she didn't remember, any of it, maybe she didn't want me to know. It's not important anyway, right now. All I can think of is my grandmother. All I can see is the moment when my grandmother had to mark the ground with a circle in the dirt around her and state her mind. And what were the words my grandmother said? Even from forty years away, they are the sweetest, clearest music I have ever, ever heard.

⋈ Chapter Sixteen ⋈

Since even Pip has given up trying to restore harmony to my grandmothers' house, it is time to take matters into my own hands. Now, I decide, while they're sitting, after another morning of worrying each other like bits of rawhide; now after they've retired, retreated, to their corners of the living room, Fanny in one of the Danish chairs, Gerda poised on the sagging edge of her cot, armed with the therapist's booklet of strengthening exercises. Pip is on the loveseat, watching a soap opera; the way her body is settled I can tell she'll leave no sooner than she'd planned. She will stay the whole week, even though she has failed in part of her mission.

"It's so nice out today," I say loudly, clearly. "I think I'll go for a drive."

Gerda looks up. Suggestions of ease of movement still annoy her. "You can take my car, then, *kind*. Where are you going?"

"I thought I'd go by the old place."

"What old place?"

"The old house. I thought I'd drive out and take a look at it."

"Why?"

"Just for old times' sake."

Gerda stares at me as if I've proposed a trip to Atlantis, to Shangri-La. "You're not thinking, Marget. There's nothing to see there. It's not our house anymore."

"Tante, what do you say—would you like to go over and have a look with me?"

"Sure." She switches the television off. "I like to see what's happening down there."

"Bah! You're crazy, both of you. It's nothing but Filipinos now, Mexicans. You'll see."

"So you can stay here, then, and keep Fan company."

"No." Gerda feels for her cane. "I'm coming with you."

"What about you, Oma?"

My grandmother shakes her head, waving her hand toward the door. "You go, you go." She's wearing a grumbling, crumbling look. Like the side of a hill that's beginning to cave.

I remember what to do.

"Well I'm not going unless Fan is going. If Fan isn't going, I don't want to go either."

My grandmother, blushing, is up and looking for her purse.

"What if I can't remember the way?" Gerda mutters. "I'm eighty-one, you know."

"I remember the way," Pip says.

"So you should sit up front with me, Tante. Gerda, why don't you and Oma sit in the back?"

"Bah."

The same yellow smell of weeds and poppies comes in through our rolled-up windows. They're all eyes, my grandmothers, and my great-aunt, as we drive between the rolling hills and down into the valley where so many square, blockish houses have filled in, pink and yellow and earth-toned. It's like looking at a bin filled with the boxes of somebody else's belongings. We nearly get lost making our way through the new, unfamiliar streets.

"Where are we?" Gerda cranes.

Pip grunts and points the way, left or right. She steers us onto the old boulevard, where the palm trees have shot up so high they look like watchtowers.

"Here!" Pip says suddenly. "Here is our street! Turn here!"

I wouldn't have known it except for the feeling that she's right, that we've come to a place, a corner, I've kept marked by a compass I didn't know I had inside my head.

I can sense disappointment rising around me.

"It's crowded."

"It's bad."

"There it is! I told you we'd find it!"

The old house is surrounded by houses, huddled in the middle. A small lot is all that's left of the large, treed piece of earth that was once wide enough to hold all of

Gerda's expectations. The ranch house is still there, elongated, sturdy in the middle, but sagging at the ends, like an overused seesaw. It's closed in all around by an ugly chain-link fence.

"Let's see if someone's home," Pip says.

"I'm not going to look."

"You two stay here, then, Gerda." I turn the engine off. "I'm going with Tante."

My aunt is already striding through the unlocked gate and toward the front door, balling her hand into a fist. I wait outside the fence, looking back at Gerda's and Fan's glum faces, hunched in profile, pouting. Not so much as a glance at each other or the house.

But surely they must see it. Surely they must recognize some of the same roses, in front. The old curve of the sidewalk up to the front door is the same, even if weeds have grown along it, untended. They must be able to see the outline of their old bedroom window, and the places where they used to set out lawn chairs and hang Christmas lights, and all the ghosts of other dead things that are now uprooted or buried. Whatever it is they don't want to look at, it must be something powerful. They stare hard away. Afraid to turn their heads toward it.

Pip comes away from the front door. "No one at home." She stands in front of me. "What should we do now?"

"Let's go around and take a look at the backyard."

"The neighbors won't like it."

"We'll stay along the fence."

178

We stay low and close together and make our way through the sideyard. I can see the three birches in my mind's eye before I see them. I conjure up their soaring, peeling, bending white trunks, the healed marks of my fingernails where I went after them, hungrily. We stand with our fingers crooked into the chain link, turning our heads and peering into our old yard. The orchard has been cut down, to make way for new houses. Pip grunts softly, shaking her head.

"It's not like it was."

"It doesn't matter, Tante."

"It's still looks the same in my head."

"Mine too."

"Look, there really is no one home."

"We could walk around back here—do you want to?"

"*Nee*. We'd better get back to the car."

We keep staring at the house. I feel sad, a little ashamed by it. But only because it's old, only because it couldn't come along with us, especially because it can't come with the one of us who will be showing up soon, in seven months, the sum of all of us now, snaking like a vine into the future. I look back and try to see my grandmothers' faces inside the car. They're only a dark blur behind the closed windows.

When I tell my mother I'm going to have a baby, she will be puzzled, unsure, she may even decide to come home. She will have to come home. Corinne will be angry with me, saying I've given in. Then she might forgive me, and buy me gifts. Pip, like a fat genie, will return, unsurprised, to the calm of her warm bottle in

Reno. My grandmothers will stare at themselves as if their fingers had suddenly grown fingers, and their toes broken out in new toes. They will forget and I will have to remind them again, they will complain and forget to be pleased.

I know people who will say I am foolish, and others who will say I am wise. And no one will know, unless I explain it to them in this way, how the past sometimes makes an answer in the future, and how balance is something we must finally find for ourselves, in our own heads, always searching for some steadying source, some reason to risk disaster, dancing on the edge of the void.

I follow Pip's bulky shoulders out to the street, the old house and yard slipping behind us. They return quietly to their old shapes, in my imagination. Pip waves to my grandmothers. I see them, all at once, leaning forward in the car, toward the closed window, almost pressing against the glass—so close together Fan's head seems to be resting on Gerda's shoulder, so tightly locked and looking toward the house they seem to be one person, held mesmerized by it. Seeing it as it is, and as they are, and as it was, and as they were. For a long moment I see my grandmothers, two heads balanced on one body. I raise my hand toward the glass, waving. But they look right through me, their ears touching as if only they can hear something, faintly, whispering, hanging in the air between them.